A startled cry from the lady Fed drew Bolan's attention

Three of his enemies were crouched behind the center vehicle in line, at least one sheltered by the Jeep on Bolan's right. He primed another grenade and lobbed it overhand, delivering the canister with accuracy born of frequent practice. It came down directly on the vehicle's flat hood and wobbled as it rolled off one side.

Three seconds...

Bolan held the Uzi level, ready to receive his adversaries when they broke to either side, his fingers resting lightly on the trigger.

Two...

One of the soldiers called a warning to his comrades, shadows stirring restlessly behind the Jeep, but when they made their move, one of the gunners picked the wrong side of the vehicle and blundered straight toward the grenade.

One...

MACK BOLAN ®

The Executioner

DON PENDLETON'S
EXECUTIONER®
HOUR OF CONFLICT

THE
★
AMERICAN
TRILOGY BOOK II

A GOLD EAGLE BOOK FROM

WORLDWIDE®

TORONTO • NEW YORK • LONDON
AMSTERDAM • PARIS • SYDNEY • HAMBURG
STOCKHOLM • ATHENS • TOKYO • MILAN
MADRID • WARSAW • BUDAPEST • AUCKLAND

First edition July 1997
ISBN 0-373-64223-7

Special thanks and acknowledgment to
Mike Newton for his contribution to this work.

HOUR OF CONFLICT

There is no place in a fanatic's head where reason can enter.
—Napoleon I

Our home-grown fanatics may be immune to reason, but they're not bulletproof. I'm about to communicate with them in the only language they seem to understand.
—Mack Bolan

To FBI Special Agent Kevin Kramer,
casualty of the Montana "Freemen" siege,
April 14, 1996. God keep.

1

You can never tell about the Badlands.

They received that nickname for a reason, after all, long years ago when travelers were heading west in wagon trains. Those early wayfarers saw something in the region that repelled and frightened them, something beyond the simple scarcity of water during summer months or the inherent risk of clashes with marauding native warriors.

There was something else.

It seemed to be the kind of land where God-fearing boys went bad somehow, turned to drinking whiskey, rustling cattle or robbing stages for the hell of it. Some of their sisters ran away to Kansas City or Chicago or St. Louis, and pursued the kind of life their parents wouldn't talk about. The Badlands were a breeding ground for outlaws and a refuge for the damned.

It takes some time for history to come full circle, but she always gets there in the end.

The target was in Rosebud County, thirty-five miles north of Forsyth. State Highway 59 would get you halfway there, but final access was by invitation only, on a private road that needed a four-wheel drive in wintertime. The entrance to the road was posted with hand-painted warning signs, and miles of barbed-wire fence surrounded the property. More signs were posted on the fence, every hundred yards or so: a simple Warning! Private Property! with skull and crossbones stenciled underneath.

No threats, per se, but none were necessary in Montana, where the right to privacy was valued next to God and mother, well ahead of apple pie.

Mack Bolan saw the signs and thought to hell with it. He had been planning to evacuate the state, but he still had some unfinished business there, and warnings posted on a fence weren't about to slow him down.

At half-past midnight on a Sunday, Bolan calculated that he had the best chance he would ever have of taking his intended quarry by surprise. The guards would be on edge, but none of the unpleasantness from Idaho had spilled across their border yet, and there was bound to be a certain sense of safety based on distance from the battle zone. On top of that, Bolan had needed almost forty hours to locate his prey, despite the help he got from Stony Man's computer data bank, and every passing moment without contact would encourage his opponents to relax.

By now, most of them would believe that they were in the clear. The killer storm had passed them by, and they could start to breathe again.

But they were wrong.

They were enjoying the deceptive calm *before* the storm, and short of running for their lives, there was little they could do to save themselves this night.

The raid wasn't a lock, of course. Nothing in life was ever guaranteed. A hundred different things could still go wrong, and Bolan could wind up dead before the night was over. But it wouldn't be from lack of laying out his strategy beforehand or committing to the strike with everything he had.

Whatever happened in the next half hour, the Executioner was going for the jugular, and if a member of the other team got lucky in the process, well, that was a risk he was prepared to take.

The road he chose to take him westward from the highway was unposted and unpaved. His adversaries didn't own the county, after all, only the thousand acres that they had transformed—on paper, anyway—into the "Free State of Montana Common Law." Their claim of local sovereignty was lame at best, a half-baked notion that arose in equal parts from misinterpretation of the U.S. Constitution and an arrogance that knew no bounds.

But Bolan wasn't interested in a political debate. He had his mind fixed on a single target, one man who could possibly advance his latest mission, put him on the track of bigger, more important prey. It had been almost two days since he started looking for that man, but Bolan had him now.

Almost.

Before the sun came up again, he meant to find out what his quarry knew.

ZEB CARTER'S MOTHER had been stuck on history when she was growing up. Her favorite characters had been the "mountain men" who struck off on their own, with little but Kentucky rifles and the buckskins on their backs to chart the Rockies, fighting hand to hand with Indians and grizzlies, blazing trails across the wild frontier. When he was born, she named him after Zebulon Pike, never once considering the ruthless teasing that he would have to take from other kids at school.

Still, it could have been worse, Carter told himself.

She could have named him Pike's Peak, after all, or even Liver-Eater, after Jeremiah Johnson, who had killed so many members of the Crow tribe to avenge his murdered wife and earned his nickname from a tendency to chow down on the dead as an expression of contempt.

At least with "Zebulon," he had a chance to knock some letters off and come up with a neutral kind of handle, one with just a touch of biblical association. With "Liver-

Eater,'' on the other hand, he would have been completely screwed.

At the moment, Carter was more interested in sacking out than changing in his identity. He had been walking post since eight o'clock, and had the better part of three more hours to go before his shift changed and relief arrived. The wind was cold that time of night out on the open plains. It got inside his jacket, through the cuffs and collar, leeching Carter's body heat no matter how he tried to readjust the woolen scarf around his neck.

And all for nothing.

The blowup out in Idaho was history by now. He was angered by what happened to his brothers in the Gem State, but the Paul Revere Militia would survive. It wasn't just some half-assed local outfit you could take out with a single punch, some gang of pimply-faced teenagers with their heads shaved, going out to beat up Jews or gays when they ran out of beer and reefer. The militia was an organized reality from coast to coast, as deadly serious as a heart attack. It was the wave of the future, America's hope for a brighter, whiter tomorrow.

That said, Zeb Carter still had doubts about the military need for him to freeze his butt off on a Sunday night.

Guard duty was a part of living at the compound, granted, one of many rules that were imposed as much for discipline as for security. Carter had learned that drill in the Marine Corps, and he understood the logic of it...but it didn't stop him bitching, even if he only muttered to himself while he was marching up and down his lonely beat.

It almost made him wish something *would* happen, just to break up the monotony and justify his shivering on the perimeter. Was it disloyal of him to think that way?

Tough.

Part of the militia creed was freedom, even if they had

to follow orders just like back in boot camp. When the smoke cleared, when the war was over, the survivors would be truly free. Carter believed that in his heart.

Still, it was boring in the wee, small hours of the morning, and he caught himself wondering if there was a better way to spend his time.

There had been some excitement, roughly twenty minutes earlier, but it had come to nothing. For a minute there, before he blinked and cleared his eyes, Carter had thought he saw a black car running with the lights off, scooting down the access road that ran a hundred yards due south of the perimeter. But a second look had shown him nothing in the way of a vehicle or telltale dust clouds.

Carter had been reaching for his plastic walkie-talkie when he caught himself, decided not to push the panic button just because his eyes were playing tricks on him. It wouldn't win him any points from the sergeant of the guard to log a phantom sighting, most especially since there was nothing they could do about the access road in any case. The unpaved track was on the Gilmer property, next door, some kind of county easement for the power lines or something, and they saw cars out there all the time.

But running dark?

Forget it. He was seeing things, a product of the darkness, the hour and his boredom. Carter kept his eyes peeled for the next few minutes, listened more intently for the sound of engines racing, but it all came down to nothing. He was starting to relax when it occurred to him that he should take a leak.

Although it was pitch-dark and he was standing on the edge of nowhere, Carter still felt hesitant about unloading in the open. Fifty yards away, in the direction he was headed, there were several stunted trees that he had previously used as a kind of makeshift rest room. They would serve him just as well tonight, he thought, as in the past.

Carter reached his destination just about the time his bladder started nagging at him in a major way, insisting that he'd better hurry up and get his business done. Unzipping, the militiaman grimaced as the chill attacked him from a new direction. He closed his eyes and listened to the whisper of his stream as it began to play across the brown, dry grass—and missed the sound of footsteps coming up behind him.

His first clue to the presence of a stranger just behind him was the sudden pressure of a hand across his mouth. It twisted sharply to the left, pain lancing through the muscles of his neck, before another kind of pain—white-hot and sharp—exploded in his throat.

In that instant, Zeb Carter knew that he was dying.

BOLAN RELEASED the sentry's deadweight, wiped his Ka-bar combat knife on the man's camouflage fatigues and slipped it back into the leather sheath suspended from his combat harness.

That was one, the first of several he would almost certainly be forced to take out before he reached his quarry. Bolan had no qualms about disposing of the enemy. He didn't revel in it, like some soldiers he had known in Vietnam and afterward, but neither did it leave him with a bad taste in his mouth or any sense of guilt.

His adversaries knew the risks involved when they picked up a gun, and if he caught the enemy napping or they underestimated him, so much the better. He would use whatever tools became available to help him do his job.

The Executioner was clad in black, a nightsuit stitched from thermal fabric that fit him like a second skin while minimizing his reaction to the early-morning chill. His combat harness and the web belt wrapped around his waist supported ammo pouches for the Colt Commando carbine slung across his shoulder and the Desert Eagle .44 Magnum semiautomatic pistol on his hip. A shoulder rig secured a second pistol—the selective-fire Beretta 93-R—underneath his left arm, with two extra magazines beneath his right. The Ka-bar combat knife was included to provide for silent kills, while half a dozen fragmentation grenades were spaced around his belt, in case the whole thing went to hell.

Whatever happened in the next few moments, Bolan wouldn't blow the strike because he had neglected to prepare and arm himself.

He checked his position with his compass, left the dead man where he lay and moved off toward the Free State of Montana's "capital." The compound proper lay a half mile north of where he stood. No lights were apparent from that distance, but he knew where he was going. Aerial photos had given him a fair idea of the camp's layout, but he would still have to seek out his target once he had penetrated the core of the hardsite.

No problem, Bolan thought as he trudged on through darkness, toward his rendezvous with death. Finding his intended quarry shouldn't be that difficult, considering the compound's size.

The real hard part, he grudgingly admitted to himself, was getting out alive.

NEAL MARTZ WAS SICK and tired of hiding out. It would be three days tomorrow, and he had a ton of work to do in Washington, around the office. He hadn't gone through a long and sometimes grueling race for Congress so that he could spend time in a Quonset hut in Rosebud County. There was nothing he could do for anyone—much less himself—while he was playing hide-and-seek with unknown adversaries in the middle of nowhere.

Not that he believed the gunmen would come after him, in any case. His Democratic opposition had referred to Martz as paranoid on more than one occasion during the campaign, and it was true that he held many views in common with the Paul Revere Militia. Hell, he was a member of the group, had been since shortly after it was founded, and while he was troubled by the killings there in Idaho, he saw no reason to assume the mayhem would be spreading to Montana. If it did, though, then the safest place for him to be was back in Washington, D.C.

Martz had his mind made up. He would leave after breakfast and drive to Billings. He could pull some strings, get on an eastbound flight from there and be in Washington by early afternoon. The local yokels didn't care much for the federal government in general, but they were still impressed by titles, in a childlike kind of way. Tell them you were a congressman or senator, and most of them would bust a gut trying to be helpful, basking in the reflected glow of someone who had made it.

Neal Martz liked the perks that went along with being sent to Washington to make the laws. He liked the fact that he could send his mail free these days, and that he couldn't be arrested while Congress was in session. Not that he was worried on that score, by any means. He had been picked up once, when he was still a kid, for driving while intoxicated—they had buried that one nice and deep during the campaign—but he was favored with a driver now and didn't have to sweat it out.

Thinking of whiskey made him wish he had some. It would help him sleep, instead of tossing on the miserable cot and staring at the ceiling of his miserable hut. This was the pits—an insult, really—and he meant to have it out with Pike as soon as possible.

Assuming Pike survived.

That was a problem, granted. Martz knew the militia leader had been injured in the recent Idaho upheaval. He was in the hospital, in serious condition, but Martz had been unable to obtain more details. He tried pulling rank, but it meant nothing to the doctors, with their oath of confidentiality and federal agents staking out the hospital.

From what he gathered on the radio and television news, the FBI had Pike's compound now—or, rather, what was left of it. Some kind of battle had been fought there, with sufficient casualties to make Dan Rather lead off with the story two nights in a row. The crucial details—who and why—remained elusive at the moment. Maybe someone in the FBI knew what was going on, but Martz wasn't about to call them and submit to questioning as if he were a suspect in the case. When he was safely back in Washington, the agents could come to *him* and ask their questions, while he kept a tape recorder running to make sure that he wasn't misquoted.

Paranoid? Not even close.

Martz knew about the different ways the Feds could set you up, discredit politicians who opposed the tax-and-spend bureaucracy in Washington. He was an adversary of the left-wing welfare state, and everybody knew it, from the White House to the IRS. They hated him for taking on the liberal establishment and speaking for the common man. They might do anything to bring him down.

And if they found him here, with the militia, that alone would be enough to give him one hellacious black eye in the media. Smart-ass reporters would connect the violence in Idaho to Martz's hiding at the compound, put him through the wringer for connections to "fanatic neo-Nazi groups," and he could spend the rest of his two years in Washington denying that he was a lunatic.

No, thank you very much.

The smart move was to split, head back to Washington, make up some crap about a brief vacation to explain his absence and—

The first explosion jolted Martz with force enough to nearly dump him off his cot. The windows of his hut rattled in their frames, the corrugated walls resounding with an echo of the blast that made him feel as if he were trapped inside a kettledrum.

He bolted to his feet, then ducked reflexively, afraid of shrapnel ripping through the walls or windows. Moving in a crouch, he proceeded toward the door, had one hand on the knob when gunfire suddenly erupted from the compound, followed quickly by another detonation.

Martz had no weapon, hadn't thought that he would need one at the compound where he was surrounded by militiamen committed to protecting him from danger. Even with a gun, he realized, he would have been as great a danger to himself as to prospective enemies. A dozen years had passed since he had last gone hunting, and he had no training whatsoever with the kind of paramilitary hardware common in the camp. He had two legs, though, and despite the fact that they were trembling, they would carry him outside, away from danger, if he wasn't spotted by the enemy and cut down in his tracks.

Who *was* the enemy? He wasted no time dwelling on the question, since it was insoluble. Survival was the first priority, and he would need a vehicle to make it work. The others could defend their compound to the death if they were so inclined.

The freshman congressman was bailing out.

Most of the vehicles were parked together, on the east side of the compound, several of them in a barnlike structure, while the rest were clustered underneath a giant camo net designed to frustrate aerial surveillance. Martz had no idea how well it worked and didn't care. He knew that the ignition keys were waiting in the vehicles, and they were kept topped off with fuel. All he would have to do was pick a ride and make a run for daylight.

He hesitated, frozen on the threshold, dredging up the courage needed for a lunge into the night where muzzle-flashes winked like lethal fireflies, bullets zipping through the darkness like mosquitoes having power to drain their victims with a single bite. Out there, the first false move would mean his death, but standing still had little more to recommend it as a plan of action.

Yet another blast, away to Martz's left, made up his mind. Another of the huts exploded, bright flames licking from the shattered windows, and a burning scarecrow vaulted through the doorway, screaming as he ran across the compound, trailing sparks.

Martz got his bearings, offered up a silent prayer and took off running toward the motor pool.

BOLAN LED the two advancing gunners by a foot or so and stroked the trigger of his Colt Commando, rattling off a stream of 5.56 mm tumblers toward the enemy. He saw the pointman stumble, like a runner caught up on a trip wire, arms outflung as if to catch himself. He went down on his face and lay unmoving in the dust.

Behind him, number two was clapping one hand to his chest, the other trying to retain a death grip on his rifle as he fell. The weapon discharged as he went on his side, a fair attempt that missed Bolan by at least a yard.

He gave the second gunner three more rounds to nail him down, and turned away to look for other targets in the fire-streaked darkness. The Executioner knew that he was running out of time, the precious moments slipping through his fingers. If he didn't find his quarry soon...

As if in answer to that thought, there was a flicker at the corner of his eye. Bolan glanced back in that direction, to his left, and saw a runner making for the motor pool, head down and elbows pumping as he ran. The man appeared to be unarmed, relying on the darkness to protect him as he made his getaway.

It could be Martz, the face that he remembered from a

public rally in Montana, no longer smug with all the answers. This guy, whoever he might be, was hellbent on escaping from the camp before someone mistook him for a pop-up target in a shooting gallery.

Bolan decided he would take the chance and turned in that direction, thankful that the muzzle-flashes of his enemies provided targets for their own comrades. The three grenades he had expended, lobbed toward different points around the camp, had caused enough confusion that the home team wasn't sure exactly what was happening, how many enemies they faced or what to do about it.

So far, he was doing fine.

The barn-garage was fifty yards to Bolan's left. The runner he was tracking got there first and hesitated for a backward glance before he ducked inside. No doubt about the ID that time.

He had found his man.

The congressman was moving toward a Jeep, one hand outstretched to grasp the handle on the driver's door, when Bolan stepped into the barn. The Executioner was too far away to tackle Martz before he slipped into the driver's seat, but he would have to slow him somehow, without resorting to a bullet. Martz was no good to him if he couldn't speak.

He took a chance.

"Yo, Congressman."

As Martz spun to face him, Bolan moved forward, taking full advantage of his quarry's obvious confusion.

"What? Oh, hey…" Martz seemed to take him for a member of the home team, trying hard to make his plastic smile seem natural, despite the circumstances. "I was looking for the sergeant of the guard."

"Nice try," Bolan said. He was close enough for Martz to see the war paint darkening his features.

"Hey, you're not—"

Bolan swung the Colt Commando's butt against his skull and took him down. A moment later, and he had Martz loaded in the shotgun seat, slumped forward, with his head below the dashboard. It wouldn't stop bullets ripping through the door, but it was still the best that he could do.

As Bolan slid behind the steering wheel and reached for the ignition key, he hoped that it would be enough.

2

It had started as a relatively simple mission, nothing Bolan hadn't done before, at least in general terms. The far-right Paul Revere Militia had been linked to several violent crimes and acts of terrorism in the States, including multimillion-dollar holdups, bombings and the assassination of a controversial talk-show host. Most recently, an undercover agent for the ATF had disappeared after he infiltrated the militia headquarters in Idaho, and then his female partner had dropped off the screen instead of coming back to base when she was summoned.

Hal Brognola's notion had involved another infiltration of the private army—this time with the Executioner on board to break the Paul Revere Militia *his* way, without tying up the courts for months or years on end or letting any of the players wriggle through a loophole in the legal net. He had been right on track before the lady Fed, one Ginger Ross, showed up alive and well and hungry for revenge. Instead of getting it, she wound up slated for some rough interrogation by the very men who'd killed her partner. Bolan had stepped in to save her life, but it had blown up in his face.

So far, he knew that Ralph Pike, founder of the Paul Reveres, was under treatment at a hospital in Idaho for injuries sustained in Bolan's blitz. If he survived, the one-time Army colonel would undoubtedly remember not to step in front of speeding Jeeps.

Pike's second-in-command, Christopher Stone, had managed to escape while Bolan was engaged with his subordinates, and he had taken Ginger with him. Bolan reckoned it was fifty-fifty, anyway, that she was dead by now, but he refused to write her off on even money. Someone had to know where Stone would run, and since Bolan couldn't reach the colonel in intensive care, he had gone looking for the next man on the totem pole.

There was a difference of opinion, in the media and law enforcement, as to how much Neal Martz really knew about the Paul Reveres. His name hadn't shown up on any list of members, granted, but he was a well-known friend of Pike and company, who spoke at public rallies for the cause and welcomed contributions from the outfit to his campaign treasury. There was a chance that he would draw a blank when Bolan questioned him, but that would be his problem. If he didn't have the information Bolan needed, it would be a toss-up whether he should live or die. In either case, the Executioner would have to find another pigeon, living with the knowledge that his time was short indeed.

He caught a break escaping from the Free State of Montana compound, probably because his adversaries had been trained to cover their superiors at any cost. In any case, they held off firing at the Jeep while Bolan cleared the compound, carrying his hostage with him into darkness, off the property and back in the direction of the access road where he had left his Blazer.

Martz was moaning, coming out of it, as Bolan parked the Jeep and came around to the passenger side. He wasn't up to fighting, though, and offered no resistance as a pair of handcuffs pinned his wrists behind his back. A double loop of duct tape sealed his lips, and Bolan dragged him over to the Blazer, dumped him on the floor behind the driver's seat and flipped a switch to activate the childproof locks that would prevent his captive from opening the back doors of the vehicle, assuming he could twist around and reach them.

Perfect.

Bolan left the headlights off as he retraced his path along the access road, connecting to Highway 59. It would be risky running dark from that point on, but the soldier saw no evidence of pursuit, and so he switched on the headlights without regret.

The thirty-five-mile run to Forsyth didn't spell the end of Bolan's journey through the predawn darkness. Passing through the Rosebud County seat, he traveled west on U.S. Highway 94, toward Billings, marking off another forty-something miles before he reached a small, run-down motel outside the little town of Nibba. Bolan had the whole place to himself, his room the last one on the end, with thirteen empties separating him from the darkened manager's office.

The Executioner parked behind the building just in case, and spent a moment making sure the congressman could walk. He left the tape and cuffs in place, dragged Martz out of the Blazer and maintained a firm grip on one of the captive's arms as they walked back to Bolan's door. Another moment, and they were inside.

Martz muttered something from behind the tape, scared-looking eyes fixed big and wide on Bolan's face. It was apparent that he didn't know why he had been extracted from the compound, and it might work best that way. The jackpot questions, when they came, would take him by surprise, let Bolan judge the prisoner's reaction if he tried to lie.

Tormented as he was by the sensation of precious time slipping through his hands, Bolan still forced himself to take his time. No matter what Martz told him, there would be no immediate results unless he found that Stone and Ginger Ross were hiding down the road in one of Nibba's several other cheap motels. For any other target, near or far, there were logistics to consider—transportation, field intelligence, supplies—and all of it took time.

The one thing Bolan didn't have to spare.

He led Martz to the bathroom, stood him in a corner by the sink and turned on the bathtub faucets, an even mix of hot and cold.

"Do you know much about statistics?" Bolan asked.

Martz looked at him as if he were insane, then shook his head.

"It's fascinating," Bolan said. "Almost sixty percent of all fatal accidents occur at home. Can you imagine that?"

Martz didn't even try to answer that one. He was staring at the bathtub, watching as it filled. A trace of steam rose from the water, prompting Bolan to adjust the temperature.

"And when those accidents occur at home," he continued, "can you imagine what the worst room is?"

Martz shook his head again, although he likely could have guessed the answer.

"It surprised me, too. I was voting for the kitchen—all those knives and open flames, all kinds of chemicals stashed underneath the sink—but kitchens came in number two. The bathroom led by almost ten percent."

Martz tried a little shrug, but wound up looking as if he suffered from a nervous tic.

"Of course," the Executioner went on, "it's logical, the more you think about it. People fall down in the shower and hit their heads. Some drown right in the bathtub—mostly children and the elderly, of course. They get their medicines mixed up and take a fatal dose of something by mistake, and you've got cleaning chemicals, just like the kitchen. Hell, a few have heart attacks each year just sitting on the toilet, straining. How's your heart there, Neal?"

Martz tried to answer, the words were muffled.

"Well, that's good," said Bolan. "I don't want you fading out on me before we have a chance to talk. I'll take the tape off in a minute. First, though, I believe you have a right to know what's going on.''

The tub was nearly full. He turned off the faucets and rose to face the congressman. Behind Martz, his reflection in the bathroom mirror showed a battle-weary soldier with his grim face painted black and green.

He looked like Death incarnate.

''Turn around,'' Bolan ordered, fishing in his pocket for a key as Martz complied, unfastening the handcuffs and depositing them on the counter near the sink.

Martz half turned toward him, reaching for the tape that sealed his lips. When Bolan hit him, swift and low, the impact folded him in two and dropped him to his knees. Martz retched behind the gag, and had to swallow hard to keep from choking on the sour bile.

''See what I mean about the bathroom?'' Bolan's voice was calm and reasonable. ''Anything can happen. Now, stand up.''

Martz made two false starts before he tottered to his feet. His face was crimson, as if he had spent the past few hours underneath a broiling desert sun.

''Take off your clothes,'' Bolan said.

A fair share of the color in his face went south at that command. Martz hesitated, measuring the odds of possible success if he resisted.

Bolan drew the sleek Beretta from his shoulder rig. ''Don't make me say 'or else,''' he cautioned.

Martz took his shirt off, braced one hand against the nearest wall as he kicked off his shoes, removed his trousers as a flush crept back into his cheeks. In boxer shorts and T-shirt, he was nothing to write home about.

''Keep going.''

With visible reluctance, trembling now, Martz stripped down to his skin. The duct tape wrapped around his lower face was all he wore as Bolan gestured toward the tub with his pistol.

"Get in."

Martz did as he was told, reacting with a grimace to the water's temperature.

"Too hot?" Bolan asked. "You'll get used to it. Sit down. Relax."

Martz lowered himself gingerly into the tub while Bolan holstered his Beretta and turned back toward the counter, where a blow drier was plugged into the wall socket above the sink, with a twelve-foot extension cord. He set the power switch at Low and raised his voice a little to be heard above the drier's whine.

"I need to ask you certain questions," Bolan said as he retraced his steps to stand beside the tub.

Martz watched him, wide-eyed, his bloodless fingers clutching porcelain.

"Before I start, though, let me tell you what I know already. That way, if the notion arises that you can lie to me and weasel your way out of this, maybe you'll think again. Okay?"

Martz nodded quickly, anxious to please.

"All right. For openers, I know what everybody knows about your visible connection to the Paul Revere Militia and its leadership. You speak at rallies for the group from time to time, most of them organized behind some front group like the Patriots for Progress or the Born-again Believers' Coalition, to preserve deniability. You're friendly with the leadership, including Pike, Chris Stone and others. The militia played a major role in funding your congressional campaign."

Martz offered no response, afraid to lie. His eyes were fixed on the drier dangling from Bolan's hand, a yard above the surface of the water that enveloped him.

"Now, for the part that never made the papers," Bolan

said. "Most of the Paul Revere Militia's contribution to your war chest came from robberies, illegal-weapons sales, some counterfeiting, this and that. Maybe you knew, maybe you didn't. My hunch is that you suspected, but you kept your mouth shut. Either way, it has to look bad in the media."

Martz shook his head, a politician's instant reflex toward denial, muttering once more behind his sticky gag.

"Wait until I'm finished," Bolan said, and let the dangling drier slip another inch.

Martz squealed and raised both hands, a naked prisoner of war surrendering.

"Now for some things I'd like to think you *didn't* know. About a month ago, your friends in the militia killed a federal agent. That's a fact. More recently, they snatched his partner for interrogation. She was at their headquarters in Idaho when it went up in smoke. Chris Stone got out alive and took her with him. Did you know that?"

Neal Martz shook his head in an emphatic negative.

"Take off the tape."

He tried his best, producing tears of pain before he got the double twist of duct tape down below his chin. His lips were red, chapped looking, and Martz grimaced at the sour taste when he licked them.

"Did you know that?" Bolan asked again.

"No! God, I swear!"

Bolan believed him. So far. "What I want from you right now," he said, "is basic information. You know Stone, his contacts."

"No, I—"

"Quiet!" Bolan let the drier slip another inch, and Martz recoiled, his effort raising breakers in the tub that lapped an inch below the hissing mouth of the appliance.

"No, please, God!"

"He doesn't hear you. I'm all you've got right now. I hope we understand each other."

"Yeah...yes!"

"All right. As I was saying, you know Chris Stone's contacts—some of them, at least—and I'm prepared to bet your life that you know where he'd go to hide if he was carrying a hostage and the dogs were snapping at his heels."

"Where would he go?"

"That's what I'm asking you," Bolan said.

"Well..."

"Take all the time you need," he said, and reeled the drier in, switching the power up to High, so that it shrieked, before he started playing out the cord again. "Take thirty seconds."

"Jesus! Wait! Stone's got all kinds of places he could run to."

"Pick the best one," Bolan told him. "Make it good."

"I'd vote for Baja," Martz suggested.

"As in Baja California?"

"Right. They've got a place down there. Not the militia, really, but a friend of theirs."

"I'm listening."

The drier hung an inch above the water, screaming like a banshee, so that Martz was forced to raise his voice as he replied.

"The place is called Colonia Cristo," Martz said. "The Colony of Christ. The guy in charge is Nehemiah Zinn. I guess you'd call him an expatriate."

"What would *you* call him?" Bolan asked.

"A nut," Martz said. "He makes the Born-Again Believers look like flaming liberals, if you want to know the truth. He moved to Baja six or seven years ago, one jump ahead of an indictment for the bombing of abortion clinics—Texas or New Mexico, I think, somewhere around in there. He's got it all worked out from Scripture that the final days are coming in the year 2000. When it happens, he's convinced that Armageddon won't be fought out in the Middle East, but down in the American Southwest. Go figure, huh?''

''What makes you think that Stone would take a hostage there?''

''Well, there's no extradition out of Mexico,'' Martz said, ''and he drops in on Nehemiah four, five times a year at least. They're up to something, maybe moving guns. I don't believe it's drugs.''

''You never asked?''

''Who wants to know that kind of shit?'' Martz asked. The standard-issue politician's tone was coming back, despite the drier dangling inches from his groin.

''I'll need coordinates,'' Bolan told him.

''Come again?''

''The colony,'' he said. ''I need it spotted on a map.''

''No problem,'' Martz replied. ''I flew down there with Pike one time myself. About two years ago, I think. One visit was enough for me.''

''How many people live there?''

''About a hundred, back when I dropped in,'' Martz said. ''I guess it could be up by now—or down. A little Nehemiah goes a long way, if you get my drift.''

''Explain.''

''Well, he's your basic zealot, with your regular messiah complex. It's his way or the highway when you join the colony. He's got more rules than Moses, everything from dietary laws to rules on sex and raising children. Some of it's Old Testament, but Nehemiah likes to customize the Scriptures every now and then.''

''You mean, he makes it up.''

''You got that right. I haven't made a study of it, but from what I hear, some of his people bailed out on him, not too long ago and started up a second colony. They're putting hexes on each other, praying for the wrath of God to smite somebody down, the whole nine yards.''

''Sounds charming.''

''Hey—'' Martz raised his hands ''—that's Zinn, not me.''

''Nice company you keep.''

''Strange bedfellows, you know?''

''And Stone hangs out there?'' Bolan asked.

''Not in the colony itself,'' Martz answered. ''The militia has a camp nearby, ten miles or so. For training or whatever.''

''Hiding from the law, you mean to say.''

''I guess.''

''Get up,'' Bolan said. As he spoke, he switched off the drier, and returned it to the counter.

Martz was dripping, trembling as he stepped out of the tub and started to reach for his clothes. Before his hand was halfway to the rumpled trousers, Bolan stopped him.

''No,'' he said. ''Wrap this around your waist.''

Martz caught the terry towel and did as he was told. ''What now?'' he asked his captor apprehensively.

Bolan retrieved a pen and notepad from the bedroom, handing them to Martz. ''Locations for the base camp and this character's so-called religious colony. I need specifics.''

Martz took several minutes, filling up two pages in the little notebook. He couldn't remember highway numbers, but there was a town called Rosarito six or seven miles west of Colonia Cristo. The militia camp lay off to the northeast.

''You'd better not be wrong,'' Bolan warned.

''It's the best that I can do.''

''Fair enough. Come on.''

''Say what?''

"We're going for a little ride."

"Like this?"

"Just hope we don't get stopped for speeding," Bolan said.

He put the handcuffs back on Martz before they left the motel room and placed his hostage in the Blazer's shotgun seat. They drove another ten miles east, toward Worden, picking up Highway 500, a state secondary road. Northbound from there, they headed toward the brooding outline of the Bull Mountains. Martz was looking nervous as the Blazer slowed some fifteen miles, by Bolan's calculation, from the nearest town.

"So, this is it," the congressman announced. His tone was fatalistic.

"Pretty much," the Executioner replied.

"What now?"

"Now you get out," Bolan said.

"What?"

"You heard me."

Bolan left his seat and moved around behind the vehicle to open Martz's door. The congressman was grumbling as his bare feet met the pavement. It was cold out, but he wouldn't freeze to death before the sun came up.

And if he did, so what?

Martz waited for the bullet. When it didn't come, and he saw Bolan turn his back, the guy regained some measure of his nerve.

"Hey, wait a minute! Are you leaving me like this?"

"You're right," Bolan said, turning back to face him. "I forgot something."

"I guess you did." Martz half turned to present the handcuffs, waiting for the key.

Bolan retrieved the motel towel instead. "That's better," he declared. "You need exposure for your next campaign."

"Goddamn it! Wait! I can't be seen like this!"

"I bet you can," Bolan said, grinning as he turned away and walked back to his open door. Martz was about to follow him, when the soldier froze him with a glare. "Don't push your luck."

Martz took the hint and stepped back to the shoulder of the highway, wincing as his foot came down on something sharp. It had to have hurt, but he was keeping quiet now.

If nothing else, the politician seemed to learn from his mistakes.

Before he drove away, Bolan rolled down his window, offering the congressman some free advice. "You'll have an urge to call your friends and tip them off," he said. "I understand the feeling. If you're smart, though, you'll resist that urge."

"I won't say anything," Martz promised.

"Because if I get the feeling that you've pulled a fast one on me, jeopardized the lady's life in any way at all, I'll have to visit you again. You wouldn't like that, Congressman. I guarantee it."

"No."

"So play it smart and keep your mouth shut, right?"

"I will."

"Good man."

Bolan could see Martz in the rearview mirror, standing naked on the roadside, as he turned the car around and headed back toward Highway 90.

It would be sometime that afternoon or evening before he got to Baja, even with some help from Stony Man. It was a gamble, leaving Martz alive, and Bolan knew he might regret it, but he was prepared to take the chance.

If he was wrong about the congressman, then he would have to live with it. But Neal Martz wouldn't have that chance.

The Executioner was moving on, but he could always double back. And if he did, there would be hell to pay.

The drive from San Diego, through Tijuana, Ensenada and the other, smaller towns, had been a long one. Bolan had crossed the border into Mexico shortly after three o'clock that afternoon and driven steadily, stopping only for gas as the sun dipped lower on the horizon. At that, it was approaching 10:00 p.m. when he pulled into Rosarito, some 420 miles due south, and he still hadn't reached his final destination for the night.

But the soldier knew where he was going, and the long drive hadn't dulled his edge. If anything, he felt keyed up, excited by the prospect of impending contact with his enemies.

And Ginger Ross.

He had no way of knowing if the lady Fed was still alive. That would require a look inside the target site itself, assuming Martz had been correct about Chris Stone's preferred escape route. If the congressman was wrong, of course, then all bets would be off.

The lady would be lost beyond recall.

If Ross wasn't at the target site in Baja, Bolan knew that he would have no second chance to track her down. There had been too much wasted time already for his liking, and as more time slipped away, the worse his chances were of ever seeing Ginger Ross again.

The woman had brought this on herself by trying to conduct a solitary operation in defiance of her orders, but he still felt obligated to retrieve her if he could and punish those responsible for her abduction, either way it went.

If all else failed, at least he meant to give Chris Stone a taste of hell on earth. It seemed the very least that he could do.

Payback was Bolan's specialty.

He topped off the Cherokee's gas tank in Rosarito, taking an old man away from his tequila in the process. Any gringo passing through the town this late was bound to cause some talk, but Bolan calculated that it wouldn't reach his adversaries' ears until the following morning, by which time it would be too late.

A full moon cast its ghostly light upon the Baja desert as he started driving east from Rosarito, Joshua trees and cactus standing gargoylelike on both sides of the narrow blacktop ribbon. He thought of Ginger Ross as he drove, and just as quickly put her out of mind. Whether the woman was alive or dead, his mission from that point would be the same: identify his enemies and raise sufficient hell to let them know that there was nowhere they could hide.

The rest, he thought, would take care of itself.

SOMETIMES JACK TRACY had to stop and look around, remind himself that he was still in Mexico. There were brief moments when he almost felt at home there, and it worried him. To Tracy's mind, that was a signal that he had been hiding out too long, and maybe he was losing it.

To start with, Tracy didn't care for Mexicans. He didn't hate their guts, exactly—not the way he did with blacks and Jews, for instance—but he looked at them as aliens, a breed apart somehow, no matter where he met them. Oh, their food was good, no doubt about it; he could never get enough of those *rellenos,* but there was a world of difference between eating in a Mexican café and living in a world where every face you saw outside the camp was brown, each voice you heard beyond the base perimeter was speaking Spanish.

Worst of all, Tracy knew *he* was the alien this time around, and that increased the feeling that he might be set upon by enemies at any moment, see his people massacred before they had a real chance to defend themselves. It was the reason that he kept the camp on full alert year-round, even before Chris Stone had come along and dropped the woman in his lap.

Of course, Tracy knew it was his own fault that he had to hide in Baja like a fugitive. Well, technically he was a fugitive, although the last he heard the FBI still didn't know his name. He had gone out one evening with a couple of those Klan boys in Missouri, and had helped them bomb a gas line south of East St. Louis. Trying to recall their reasons, all he could remember was the taste of whiskey and a dare that he couldn't refuse. It wasn't a militia project, but he told himself it made no difference. Who would ever know?

As it turned out, the dynamite they used was stolen from an Army base in Indiana, and the Feds were tracking it before the bomb went off. Now his companions from the triple-K fraternity were doing time with mud people, while Tracy cooled his heels in Baja, waiting for the day he could go home.

At least Stone let him run the compound while he waited, riding herd on thirty-five or forty Paul Revere militiamen who had been forced to leave the States on one beef or another. He had bail-jumpers, jail-breakers, two or three under indictment for assorted felonies at home and six or seven so-called deadbeat dads, who had elected to display their contempt for the Jew-dominated government by ignoring child-support orders from the left-wing family courts. They weren't the best team he had ever worked with by a long shot, but the setup still beat hiding out in Baja on his own.

And now he had the woman to distract him.

She was fine—no doubt about it. Tracy had not sampled any of her goodies yet, but it was on his mind to speak with Stone about that little matter in the morning. She was nothing but a prisoner—there were no plans to ransom her or send her home, alive or otherwise—and Tracy couldn't understand why she should be off-limits to the troops. As their commander, he would naturally expect to be the first in line. Or maybe second, after Stone, if that was what it took to get the cold-eyed bastard on his side. Whatever, there was no point he could see in handling her like a princess, when anyone with an ounce of sense knew she would never be released alive.

If Stone released her, she would make her way back to the States, file charges—kidnapping, at least—and Stone would be the man without a country, maybe even horning in on Tracy's job as leader of the Baja compound. That would never do, and Tracy meant to head the problem off before it got too close and gathered such momentum that it plowed him under like a road apple.

In fact, he thought, he might even drop in on the woman and have a little chat with her right now. Why not? Stone might be angry, but what exactly could he do? Exile the men who were already exiles? Put them on report? Take them out and shoot them, one by one? In realistic terms, there wasn't much he could do, other than raise hell, and Tracy had a feeling that Stone wouldn't really mind that much if something happened to the federal femme. Hell, it might even come as a relief.

He had his mind made up to check it out, was working up the nerve to make his move when thoughts of steamy, stolen sex were driven from his mind by the explosive sound of autofire. Tracy picked out the rattle of a 9 mm subgun, followed quickly by the sound of a Kalashnikov, then two. A semiauto pistol chimed in with the chorus, sounding like a puppy yapping at the big dogs, trying to ingratiate itself.

Tracy scooped up his .45 as he was moving toward the door, thought better of it and went back to get his M-16 A-1. He hoped the problem was a nervous sentry, firing at the desert shadows and provoking others to do likewise, but you couldn't be too careful in a foreign country, when you knew that there were enemies on every side. Between the hassles he had lived through in the last six months, and the more recent blowup in the States, Jack Tracy trusted no one but himself, his trigger finger and the weapon in his hand.

THE CAUSE OF BOLAN'S trouble was a young militiaman with kidney problems, coming back from the latrine. Apparently the inmates of the compound packed their weapons everywhere—at least, this one was packing—and it only took a heartbeat for him to decide that Bolan was a stranger with no rightful business in the camp. Instead of calling out a warning to his friends on guard, the young man grabbed the submachine gun that was dangling at his right hip on a shoulder strap, and swung the muzzle toward his target, index finger tightening around the trigger as he made his move.

The Uzi Bolan carried had been fitted with a sound suppressor. His 3-round burst was audible, if you were close enough and listening, a sound like ripping canvas. All three rounds were dead on target, drilling through the young man's rib cage, slamming him backward and down to the ground. But there was nothing the Uzi could do about his trigger finger, or the dying reflex that produced a spasm in his muscles, squeezing off a wild burst as he fell.

His weapon was an Ingram M-10, chambered in .45 caliber, with a cyclic rate of fire approaching 1,200 rounds per minute. At that rate, the stubby SMG's 32-round magazine was emptied in a second and a half, and the report was loud enough to wake the dead.

So much for subtlety.

The good news was that Bolan had his target spotted. He had already completed one full circuit of the camp before he met his nemesis at the latrine, and there was only one hut in the compound with a hasp and padlock on its single door. The size of it told Bolan that it wouldn't be much good for storage, unless the militiamen were stashing microchips. That led to the conclusion that there might be someone locked inside, rather than something they were trying to protect from prying eyes or sticky fingers. Someone who would otherwise attempt to run away. A prisoner.

Like Ginger Ross.

Of course, Bolan could be wrong. The locked hut might turn out to be the brig, or someone's private liquor stash. In truth, it could be anything, but Bolan needed focus at the moment, something in the nature of a concrete target, and the locked hut was the best that he could do.

Now all he had to do was break into that hut, discover who or what was kept there and slip out of camp—with Ginger Ross, if possible—before his adversaries got their act together and began to make their wild shots count.

He palmed a frag grenade, released the safety pin and hurled the bomb toward the far side of the compound, where a generator chugged away inside a clapboard shack. The detonation, when it came, took out the front wall of the building, shrapnel ripping through the generator wires, fuel tank and engine housing, bringing instant darkness to the camp.

By that time, several sentries were unloading aimlessly into the darkness, while their comrades scrambled out of plywood barracks, trying to discover what in hell was going on. Bolan engaged a couple of his nearest adversaries, chopped them down with silenced Uzi rounds, then grabbed a folding-stock Kalashnikov from one of them as he moved on.

If he was right about the prison hut, and Ginger Ross was locked inside, the lady Fed would need a weapon for their getaway. He didn't know if she was checked out on the AK-47, but it was a fairly basic weapon, and he had no time to pick and choose. He slung the rifle, feeling it slapping at his left hip as he ran. The Uzi in his hands was ready for all comers, Bolan's answer to whatever challenge might arise.

The shack he had in mind had been unguarded on his first pass, but there seemed to be some kind of fallback plan in place. Two sentries had appeared from somewhere, both armed with Kalashnikovs, to stand on each side of the padlocked door.

Bolan rushed the gunners from their left, surprising them despite the fact both were on alert. They were distracted by the chaos on the far side of the camp, where Bolan's frag grenade had detonated, and they didn't see him coming until he was close enough to use the SMG.

And by that time, it was too late.

His first rounds took the nearer sentry, ripping through his side and spinning him before he realized he was in danger, the explosive impact driving him against the stout wall of the shack. As he fell, his sidekick pivoted to face the unexpected threat, his AK-47 leveled from the hip.

He almost made it, but the Uzi beat him there, a short stroke on the trigger sending half a dozen rounds to stitch neat holes across his chest and slam him backward in the dust. At least one of the bullets struck his rifle, plucking it from his hands as he went down. The young man's body was still twitching as the Executioner stood over him and turned his full attention to the padlocked door.

He had one chance, and he could hear the game clock running in his head. A few more moments, and he would be moving into sudden-death overtime.

The Executioner raised his submachine gun, aiming at the lock.

HER BRIEF INTERROGATION at the Paul Revere Militia compound should have been the worst of it for Ginger Ross, but things had only gotten worse since then. Stone and the others hadn't laid a hand on her, other than to guide her roughly from point A to point B, when they had her blindfolded, but Ross would have chosen pain over the sheer uncertainty and dread that dogged her every waking moment.

She didn't relish the idea of torture, but at least it would have been a break from the monotony of waiting, never knowing if the next time she heard footsteps coming toward the hut, it might turn out to be her executioner.

They couldn't let her live: that much was obvious to anyone with half a brain—which, she suspected, would include approximately half of the militiamen whom she had met so far. She had been blindfolded a lot of the time during transit, but this new location was someplace hot and dry. A desert, she decided, though she couldn't tell which desert. From their travel time, the long trip down, it could have been anywhere in the American Southwest or northern Mexico.

The problem was she knew Chris Stone and had enough on him to put him in the chair for kidnapping if he released her. There could be no doubt that she would do exactly that; it would have been a waste for her to beg and plead, try making Stone believe that she would be so grateful for her life that she would suddenly be stricken with amnesia where her ordeal was concerned.

The number two man in the Paul Revere Militia wouldn't

buy that line, nor would his various subordinates, who stared at her when they got the chance as if she were the sweet dessert for some elaborate banquet they had planned. None of them tried to hide his face, and the breakdown in security told Ross she was definitely marked to die.

Escape would be her only hope, and there was little she could do in that regard. No, scratch that. There was nothing she could do to help herself. The bastards had her shackled to her cot, and while the cot itself was light enough to lift and move around her cell, it would have been impossible for her to carry it while she was running for her life.

As far as weapons were concerned, she was restricted to the cot and a stainless-steel bucket that served as her toilet. The bucket was emptied twice a day by a young man carrying an automatic rifle. Ross guessed that she could throw the reeking contents in his face next time he came to fetch it, and attempt to bean him with the bucket, but the price of failure could be death. Besides, if she succeeded in disabling him, she would still be shackled to the cot, unable to escape.

Her mind was racing, grasping at straws. If she *was* able to overpower her guard, then she would have his weapon. She could blast the chain off, make a break for it and try to take several of the bastards with her before she was cut down.

Forget it.

She was trained to handle a variety of weapons, but she didn't qualify as a one-woman army. Outnumbered as she was, she didn't stand a chance of blasting her way out.

And suppose she did? What then?

Without a decent fix on her location, she couldn't evade pursuit or even call for help, if by some miracle she reached a telephone. A road sign would be useful, but she had to reach a highway first, and God knew how long that would take. With armed pursuers on her trail, she wouldn't stand a chance.

Still, she would fight before she let them kill her like a helpless animal. The honey bucket was her only weapon, and the chain around her leg was long enough to let her reach it without picking up the cot to drag it after her. She would use it as a last resort, when they came to kill her. At least she would have the satisfaction of knowing that one of the triggermen had a sour taste in his mouth.

When the shooting started, Ross was taken by surprise, confused, wondering what it could mean. There were too many weapons blasting all at once for it to be a simple accident or nervous sentry, and the sound of an explosion made it sound as if the Paul Reveres had a pitched battle going on.

At once, she thought of Mike Belasko and the firefight that had saved her from interrogation back in Idaho. Had that been his show? And if so, was there some way he could have followed her? Who else would even make the effort?

Ross bolted to her feet as something heavy slammed against the front wall of the shack beside the door. A body falling? There were scuffling sounds outside, the chugging sound of an automatic weapon fitted out with a sound suppressor.

"Stand back from the door," a familiar voice ordered.

She did as she was told, retreating to the cot and dropping to a crouch, hands lifted to protect her face.

THE PADLOCK WAS a stout one, but a burst from Bolan's Uzi tore the hasp completely off its mounting, and the door swung open as he shouldered it aside. Ross peered at him through upraised hands, hunched beside a steel-framed cot. One ankle was secured to the bed frame by a cuff and a five- or six-foot length of chain.

No key.

"Move over there," he said, guiding the woman toward a point that stretched the chain full length between her slender ankle and the cot. "And turn your face away."

He stepped in close, the bulky muzzle of the Uzi's suppressor mere inches from the chain. His first shot bent the target link, and two more ripped it open, leaving Ross with the iron around her ankle, trailing three links on the floor.

"Best I can do," he said, "under the circumstances."

"I'll get by. Can we go now?"

"That's the plan." He handed her the rifle he had liberated from its owner. "Are you qualified on this?"

"Just watch me," the agent said, and flashed the first smile he had ever seen adorn her face.

"Okay. We're on the east side of the camp, near the perimeter. My vehicle is two miles south, but there's no way for us to reach it if we've got a hunting party on our heels. We'll need a ride."

"They have some Jeeps outside," she told him, pointing toward the north end of the camp. "Some motorcycles, too, I think."

"I saw them coming in. That's where we're going first. You with me?"

"Try and stop me."

The Executioner was turning toward the open doorway when a gunner stuck his head inside. One glimpse of Bolan and the hostage, and he went wide-eyed, sucking in the breath to give a warning shout some volume.

Bolan shot him in the face and blew him backward through the doorway. Ross gasped but made no other sound as Bolan stepped across the threshold, trusting her to follow him.

As if she had a choice.

Two Paul Reveres were closing in a rush, and Bolan swung to face them as they opened fire, not aiming, trusting an erratic spray of slugs to do the job. He took his time and shot the nearer of them in the chest and dropped him in a headlong sprawl. The second shooter was attempting to decide which target he should fire on, when two rounds from Ross's rifle tore into his gut and put him down.

"Come on!"

The Jeeps were lined up side by side, with no keys in evidence. Rather than searching for them, maybe wasting time to hot-wire one of the vehicles, Bolan chose a foreign-model dirt bike, climbed aboard, pressed the starter and kicked it into life. Ross got on behind him, one arm wrapped around his waist, the other clinging to her AK-47.

"Ready?" Bolan asked her.

"Go, for God's sake!"

The soldier went, the bike's engine whining. Ross gripped his web belt, near the buckle, and pressed close against him. She had the AK-47's sling across her shoulder, but the weapon's weight still put strain on her arm.

Defiantly he switched on the motorcycle's headlight and opened up the throttle, running with the desert wind warm in his face. Someone was firing at them, and Ross fired back, but Bolan concentrated on his driving, knowing that a crash would be their death. Militiamen flashed past him, left and right, some diving to escape the headlight's beam. In front of him, the open desert raised a wall of darkness to receive him.

Bolan rushed to meet it like a long-lost friend.

4

"Goddamn it, hurry up!" Jack Tracy's rage had given him a pounding headache, and he tried to vent some of the pain by shouting at his troops, demanding greater speed, less awkward gawking at the shambles of their camp.

Tracy couldn't afford to count the cost just yet. He had lost several men; that much was obvious. A number of their bodies could be seen from where he stood, beside one of the Jeeps. The generator shack was virtually demolished, and they had no power in the camp. Pale flashlight beams and Jeep headlights provided sparse illumination as his men attempted to recover from the hit-and-run assault.

The woman was no longer in the shack, but there were two dead guards outside, and the shattered lock and a length of chain still fastened to her cot told Tracy that she had been rescued by a pro. All this to steal the bitch, and it made Tracy wonder if she might be something special after all.

The answer to that question would be waiting for him in the desert, if the chosen members of his chase team ever got their act together. They were piling into Jeeps now, but it seemed to take forever, their escapee and her rescuer increasing their lead with each moment that passed.

At least he knew that there were only two of them. The witnesses were clear on that much, and there was no way for three to ride the dirt bike they had stolen. Granted, there might still be others waiting for them in the desert, but Tracy knew that he would have to take that chance.

Stone would go crazy when he heard about the woman. It wasn't far-fetched to think that he might execute the man or men he deemed responsible for her escape. He wouldn't hesitate to put a slug in Tracy's brain, appoint a new commander for the camp to do things his way.

Tracy had to retrieve the woman and deal with her companion now, while there was time to save himself. That way, at least, despite the fact of her escape, Stone had to see that Tracy was swift and strong enough to deal with any situation that arose.

"Get in the fucking Jeep!" he bellowed at a straggler, nodding to his driver even as he spoke. His Jeep, the first of three, surged forward, headlights picking out the dirt bike's track as they left camp and started out across the wasteland.

Fucking Baja. Tracy had despised it since he got there, but the grim terrain might help him now. The bike was built for speed and off-road travel, but its driver wouldn't be familiar with the landscape. With some luck, he might crash into an arroyo, maybe break his neck and save Tracy the hassle of killing him.

As for the woman, he supposed he ought to hope they got her back alive for Stone's sake, but as far as Tracy was concerned, all bets were off. She owed him blood, for the young men who had been killed in her escape. It wouldn't break his heart if she was "accidentally" gunned down by one of his subordinates. In fact, Tracy thought, he might do the job himself.

Stone couldn't fault him there, since everybody knew that Stone himself would kill the woman, in time. It was a given. Tracy would be moving up the timetable, but not by much.

"Can't you go any faster?" he snapped at his driver.

"Not unless you want to break an axle, sir," the wheel-man answered.

"Shit!"

It felt as if they were creeping until Tracy glanced away to one side or the other and saw the Joshua trees and cacti passing in a blur. That wasn't right, of course—the trees weren't passing him—but that was how it felt to Tracy, as if he were standing in the eye of a hurricane, watching the catastrophic wind swirl around him, knowing it was his turn next.

The ground was rough, the Jeep's tires slamming over rocks and rutted soil that baked as hard as concrete in between infrequent rains. On those occasions when it did rain, water seemed to fall in torrents on the harsh, unyielding land and turned arroyos into roiling rivers that could sweep away a man—or car—and swallow him without a trace.

No rain tonight, though, and the three-Jeep convoy made fair time. They could have traveled faster if the dirt bike's taillight had been visible, but picking out the tracks took longer, slowed them.

Tracy hoped the bastard enjoyed it while he could. Pursuit was hard on his heels, and there was nowhere he could hide.

THE BIKE RAN OUT of gas when they were three miles out. Bolan had begun to circle eastward, working his way back around to the site where his own vehicle was parked, but they would never make it now. Not on the bike, at any rate.

He had been conscious of the leaking, bullet-punctured gas tank even as they cleared the hostile camp, but there was nothing to be done about it. One leg of his nightsuit was soaked through with gasoline; it stung his flesh and reeked with fumes that would have flared at once had anyone been rash enough to strike a match. In lieu of stripping,

Bolan knelt and scooped up two handfuls of sand, rubbing the grit into his soggy pant leg.

"This is bad," Ginger Ross commented.

"Could have been worse," he answered, thinking that the bullet could as easily have pierced his back or hers. They could be dead now, maybe stripped and dumped into a shallow grave, instead of standing underneath the stars and talking while a hunting party followed on their trail.

It never crossed his mind that Stone's militiamen would let the woman go without attempting to retrieve her. He had no idea of how they were at tracking in the desert, whether they could even find the bike's trail prior to sunrise, but he knew that standing still was tantamount to suicide.

"Come on," he said when he had checked his compass. "Where?"

"That way," Bolan told her, pointing. "It's a hike, but we can still get to my car if no one stops us on the way."

"Terrific. That's an 'if' to die for."

"If you'd rather wait right here, my guess is that they won't be long."

"No, thanks."

They had been walking for perhaps five minutes when he heard the sound of vehicles approaching from the rear. Too soon, he told himself, but knew there could be no one else out here at this time of night. He paused and glanced back toward the point where they had left the dirt bike. Counting headlights, he made out three vehicles—the Jeeps—and calculated four men to a ride. Say five, if they were extracautious and determined.

Twelve to fifteen guns against their two, and even knowing Ross had the guts to kill a man, it would make no great difference if their adversaries caught them in the open.

"We need cover," Bolan said. "Start looking."

"I *am* looking. If we had lights, maybe I— Shit!"

He swung around to find her, but the lady Fed was no-where to be seen. It was as if the earth had opened up to swallow her alive.

"Where are you?" Bolan whispered, afraid to raise his voice with enemies so close at hand.

"Down here," she answered in a voice that sounded far away.

He trailed the sound and found himself standing on the lip of another arroyo, one of those rain-washed gullies that scarred the desert like marks from some ancient whipping with a giant's flail. Ross had missed it in the darkness, stepped over the edge and slid six feet or so on her backside before she came to rest at the bottom.

"Goddamn cactus!" She was fuming, working up a head of steam.

"Relax," Bolan said, crouching as he scrambled down to join her. "You just found our cover. What's a little wounded pride?"

"WE'VE GOT them now."

Jack Tracy kicked the useless dirt bike, grinning fiercely. In the bright glare of his own Jeep's headlights, he could see the bullet hole in one side of the motorcycle's fuel tank. Just a few more inches, and it would have burrowed into flesh. He would be looking at a dead man now instead of at a machine.

No matter.

Somewhere in the darkness up ahead, the woman and her would-be savior were on foot, outnumbered and out-gunned. They could not travel far, and there was no way in the world they could outrun three Jeeps on open ground.

No way at all.

The trick, he realized, would be in picking up their tracks and following along until they made the kill. His quarry would be moving slower now, but they would also make less noise, leave fewer traces of themselves behind, and there would be no hope of glimpsing brake lights in the distance if the trail began to fade.

"Let's move!" he snapped, returning to the Jeep and settling in beside his driver.

"Which way?" asked the man behind the wheel.

"The same way we've been going," Tracy said, making no effort to disguise his anger. "What, you think they turned around and passed us going back the other way?"

"Just asking," the wheelman said, and remembered in the nick of time to add a "sir" for military courtesy.

The Jeep rolled on, the others fanning off to either side and hanging back a little, in a rough triangular formation, headlights burning tunnels in the desert night. A few more moments, Tracy told himself, and they would spot the woman staggering along, with her anonymous protector at her side. He wouldn't tolerate the thought of either one escaping. It would cost him too much when Chris Stone returned and was informed of the events. This way, at least, Tracy could prove his skill at coping with adversity. There would be heat enough to go around, but no one could accuse him of dropping the ball twice in a row.

The only question now was how long it would take to run down the targets. The dirt bike was his landmark; its location told him everything he had to know about the general direction they were traveling. Of course, there was a lot of desert out there, hiding underneath the cloak of night, but Tracy had to trust in luck to some degree. Without that hope, he might as well turn back right now, bug out before Stone made it back—or maybe shoot himself to save a firing squad the trouble.

One thing about the desert—this far out in Baja, there was nowhere to run, no place to hide. If he was forced to push the search past dawn and let the broiling sun become his ally, baking those he sought in their own juice before he ran them down, so be it. Tracy was committed to pursue them for however long it took. Under no circumstances would he fail. It was unthinkable.

They seemed to drive for hours after stumbling on the motorcycle, but a quick glance at his watch showed Tracy that a mere five minutes had elapsed. When he looked back, he couldn't see the dirt bike, but he had a feeling that they hadn't traveled all that far, perhaps no more than half a mile. At this rate, it would take forever to retrieve the woman and her unknown friend.

"Oh-oh."

The driver's tone was ominous. Tracy glanced at him, then peered out through the dusty windshield, following the headlight beams out to their limit. There, just at the far edge of the lights, it seemed as if the earth stopped short and fell away into a kind of void.

"What's that?" he asked the driver.

"An arroyo, looks like. If it's more than two or three feet deep, we'll have to go around."

More wasted time, Tracy thought, biting off a curse before it passed his lips. An obstacle that blocked the Jeeps would block his quarry, too. Unless...

"We'd better check it out," he said to no one in particular. "They could be hiding in there." When no one moved, he swiveled toward the two men seated in the back and said, "Go on, for Christ's sake! Have a look."

The two militiamen climbed down without complaint, one on each side of the Jeep, and moved toward the arroyo with their weapons at the ready. They were backlit by the headlights of the other vehicles, and Tracy thought of switching off the lights to keep from offering their silhouettes as targets. But if the lights went out, how would the pointmen see what they were doing?

Screw it.

It was probably a waste of time in any case. What kind

of idiot would crawl down in a hole and wait for his pursuers to arrive? It made no sense when they could keep on running, put more ground between themselves and those who hunted them. An adversary smart enough to steal the woman out of Tracy's camp would certainly keep moving under cover of the night. The other option—sitting still and waiting for the ax to fall—was tantamount to suicide.

But Tracy felt obliged to check it out, regardless. Just in case.

The pointmen had advanced some fifty feet, and had another ten or fifteen feet to go before they reached the lip of the arroyo. Tracy knew the headlights wouldn't help them then. It would be dark down in the hole. How would they see if anyone was hiding there?

He had a flashlight in the glove compartment, and was just about to call one of the soldiers back to get it when all hell broke loose. At first, the muzzle-flashes seemed to be an optical illusion, unaccompanied by any sound of gunfire, but there was no doubt about their impact as his soldiers started jerking, twitching, spouting jets of crimson from the wounds that seemed to magically appear. Both men were down before Tracy found his voice.

"Incoming!"

It was all that he could think of as he ducked beneath the dashboard, groping for his holstered pistol, praying it wasn't too late to save the play.

To save himself.

GINGER ROSS WAS ready when Belasko dropped the pointmen, squeezing off two short bursts from his Uzi submachine gun. She expected a reaction from the others, without knowing the exact form it would take. She held the liberated AK-47, its folding stock extended and braced against her shoulder, and was peering over open sights. Her index finger curled around the weapon's trigger, taking up the slack.

Somebody shouted, "Incoming!" and gunfire sputtered from the Jeeps. Ross couldn't have said how many guns were firing, and it hardly mattered. One would be too many if the bastards scored a lucky shot.

And if they killed Belasko, if they managed to disarm her, it would mean a trip back to the desert compound, where her death by slow degrees was guaranteed. Better to fight and die right here, she thought, than to submit and make her final living hours one long scream of agony.

She found a target, sighting on the nearest Jeep, and stroked the AK-47's trigger. Half a dozen bullets rattled off downrange, the weapon kicking back against her shoulder with more force than she remembered from her training sessions years ago. The ATF used M-16s, which featured less recoil than the Kalashnikov, and she readjusted her grip on the rifle for better control. The second burst was better, and she was rewarded with a sound of breaking glass as one of the Jeep's headlights winked out, cracks sprouting on its windshield.

A couple of the gunners had her spotted, firing at her muzzle-flashes, bullets whizzing overhead, some kicking dirt in Ross's face. She held her breath and squinted through her lashes, firing back. One of her enemies was punched backward by a bullet in the chest, arms flailing as he fell.

Her footing was the problem now. It was a challenge, clinging to the sandy wall of the arroyo, bracing with her toes, knees, elbows, when the soil kept trying to shift out from under her and drop her to the rough floor of the desert gully. She had made that journey once already, and she wasn't looking forward to an instant replay, most particularly when she had a war to fight upstairs.

Two running figures broke clear of the nearest Jeep, one

silhouetted briefly in the headlights, crossing over, while his sidekick scuttled through the shadows. They were trying to outflank her, looking for a way into the long arroyo that would let them come up on her right and take her by surprise. One of their friends provided cover fire, but it was high and wide, the bullets passing two or three feet over the woman's head.

She tracked the runners, leading them and waiting for the perfect moment, knowing that if she delayed too long, the mere rotation of her body might propel her to the bottom of the gorge. Another heartbeat, just one more...

She squeezed the AK-47's trigger and rattled off a long burst with the forward runner in her sights, sweeping across him toward the second gunman, lifting off the trigger only when she got results. The first man stumbled, went down in an awkward shoulder roll and didn't rise again. The other was about to leap across his fallen comrade when a hot round took him in the armpit, slammed him over sideways to sprawl in the dirt.

Ross swung back in the direction of the strike team, fired off half a dozen rounds—and cursed with feeling as the rifle's hammer fell upon an empty chamber. She was out of ammunition, and the single magazine was all she had.

She popped the empty magazine, discarded it and thought about her problem. There were more guns, and replacement magazines, beside the bodies of the two men she had killed, no more than twenty yards away. It would be relatively simple to run out there, grab a bandolier or two and dash back to the gully.

Right. With every gunman in the hunting party firing at her, nothing in the way of cover and no way for Belasko to protect her. Still, she couldn't bring herself to let it go without at least attempting to defend herself.

Ross was gathering her nerve to make the run, feet digging in, the muscles bunching in her arms and shoulders, when a bullet struck the earth in front of her and sprayed grit in her eyes. She yelped, lurched backward and was airborne in a heartbeat, plunging toward the rocky bottom of the wash.

BOLAN LOBBED the frag grenade downrange and resumed firing with his suppressed Uzi, dropping another militiaman in his tracks before the lethal egg exploded underneath the last Jeep on his left. Hot shrapnel found the gas tank, and a secondary blast engulfed the vehicle, a lake of fire spreading rapidly around the crippled four-wheel drive. A pair of ghastly human torches danced and capered in the flames before collapsing into death.

A startled cry from Ross brought his head around, and Bolan saw her tumbling down the side of the arroyo, landing in a heap below. She scrambled to her feet, already cursing, and he turned his full attention back to those who meant him mortal harm. The lady Fed would have to take care of herself for now.

How many guns remained on the other team? Assuming there were twelve to start with, then their number had to have been reduced by two-thirds at the very least. Ross had dealt with three that he was sure of, while his bullets and grenade had claimed no less than five. Say four survivors, then—or maybe seven, if the Jeeps had carried five men each.

Three of his enemies were crouched behind the center vehicle in line, at least one sheltered by the Jeep on Bolan's right. To flush out the main group, he primed another grenade and lobbed it overhand, delivering the canister with accuracy born of frequent practice. It came down directly on the Jeep's flat hood and wobbled as it rolled off to one side.

Three seconds...

Bolan held the Uzi level, ready to receive his adversaries

when they broke to either side, his finger resting lightly on the trigger.

Two...

One of the soldiers called a warning to his comrades, shadows stirring restlessly behind the Jeep, but when they made their move, one of the soldiers picked the wrong side of the vehicle and blundered straight toward the grenade.

One...

Bolan squinted as the frag grenade went off, its shrapnel ripping through the startled gunman's body, shredding him before the shock wave blew him backward in a spray of liquid crimson, painting one side of the Jeep and leaving blotches on the sand. If he had time to scream before he died, the sound of it was lost in the explosion that destroyed him.

The Executioner swung his SMG to greet the others as they broke from cover on the far side of their vehicle, both sprinting for the final Jeep in line. He cut the pointman's legs from under him and kept on pumping bullets as the runner fell across his line of fire, the parabellum manglers flipping him as if some unseen hand had used a giant spatula.

The second runner nearly made it, but his nerve failed at the final instant and he faltered, breaking stride. His hands were raised, as if to block a lightning strike from heaven, when the stream of bullets tore into his rib cage, pulping heart and lungs, the impact twirling him around to drop him on his back.

And that left one.

The sole survivor of the hunting party knew he was in trouble. He was looking for an out but couldn't find one, with his lifeless comrades littering the desert sand around him. There were two Jeeps burning now, and they provided all the light that Bolan needed as he climbed out of the gully, moving toward the last vehicle in a fighting crouch.

The last militiaman could probably have bought himself some time by staying where he was and making each shot count, but he was on the verge of losing it, unnerved by the disaster that had claimed his friends. Instead of staying put, he rose from cover, fired a short burst from the hip and started running back in the direction he had come from, elbows pumping, sobbing gasps of effort bursting from his lips.

It was too easy, but the Executioner couldn't allow him to escape. A 3-round burst from under fifty feet drilled into the target, pushing him into a boneless sprawl, face in the dirt, his weapon spinning clear of lifeless fingers. Bolan scouted the perimeter, made sure he wasn't overlooking anyone, then doubled back to check on Ross in the gully.

"I ran out of bullets," she informed him as she crawled up into view.

"You've got no shortage of replacements," he replied.

"I see that." She was looking at the third Jeep, though, her face set into a thoughtful frown. "Will that thing run?" she asked.

"Somebody shot out the headlights and the windshield," Bolan said, "but it couldn't hurt to try."

"Beats walking, anyway," she replied, and trailed him toward the Jeep. Along the way, she paused to strip one of the bodies of its bandolier, reloading her Kalashnikov, the belt of spare mags draped across her shoulder.

Bolan slid into the driver's seat and tried the key. It worked. He put the Jeep in gear and pointed it in the direction of his waiting vehicle.

So far so good, he thought.

But they were still a world away from home.

5

"I don't believe this shit!"

Christopher Stone was livid, pacing through the ruins of his camp, with half a dozen young militiamen strung out behind him, looking apprehensive and cringing slightly when he turned to glare at them.

"You're telling me one man did this?" When no one answered, Stone shouted at them, "*Speak* to me, goddamn it!"

"Yes, sir," said the oldest of the group, a blonde with sergeant's stripes on one sleeve of his camouflage fatigues. The other sleeve was gone, and a dirty bandage was wrapped around his upper arm. "At least, one's all we saw, sir."

"And he took off on a motorcycle with the woman?"

"Right, sir. Headed east, he was. That's when Lieutenant Tracy took the others out to run them down. Three Jeeps, a dozen men."

"And Tracy never made it back." Stone's voice was flat now, as if all his rage had been exhausted looking at the bodies lined up under camo tarps, the flattened generator shack, the other odds and ends of chaos in the compound.

"No, sir," the young sergeant answered.

"That's going on eight hours now," Stone said. "And no one's gone to look for him, I take it?"

"No, sir. We, uh, that is, he instructed us to wait till he came back."

"At some point, did it cross your mind that he was dead, for Christ's sake? Did you ever think that maybe he's not coming back?"

His voice had risen to a shout once more, and the six men stepped back a pace, almost as if they had rehearsed the move before he got there.

"Sir, we—"

"Forget it! We'll assume there are another dozen dead out there somewhere, with three Jeeps that can be traced back to us. And all the gear they carried with them—guns, ammo, you name it. Someone has to check it out ASAP, before the goddamn *federales* stick their noses in and show up asking questions. Understood?"

"Yes, sir, but who?"

"You've got the stripes," Stone said. "In Tracy's absence, that makes you the man. Am I correct?"

"Well, sir…"

"Don't weasel on me, son. It takes a *man* to do this kind of work, not some pathetic snot-nosed kid. I'm guessing that you had to earn those stripes. They weren't just handed to you on a silver platter. Am I right?"

"Yes, sir!" The blonde's pride kicked in, with his buddies watching to find out how he would handle it.

"Well, then, you've got a job to do. Take one Jeep, three men you can trust and find out what the hell's gone down with Tracy's team. I'll tidy up around the camp and take the rest of the survivors out of here before the law shows up."

"Out where, sir?"

"Back to Colonia Cristo," Stone said. "It's all we've got right now."

"But, sir—"

"Are you questioning my orders, Sergeant?"

"No, sir!"

"I sincerely hope not, boy, because from where I stand,

you've got a loaded plate already. Adding me to your list of problems would be a serious mistake. Are we clear on that point?''

"Crystal, sir!''

"Then get moving, goddamn it! You're wasting my time.''

Stone hadn't counted on returning to the colony this soon, but then again, he hadn't counted on the woman's escaping, either, killing nearly half his soldiers in the process. No, scratch that. The killing had been done by someone else. One man, according to his troops, if Stone could trust their word and eyesight. One man who apparently had also dealt with Tracy and his chase team somewhere in the desert outside camp.

"I don't believe this shit!'' Stone said again, to no one. Everywhere he looked, the camp was in a shambles. It had never been that much to look at, granted, but the place was a disaster area this morning. He was gone one night, and it had gone to hell.

A little voice inside him said that he should be grateful for small favors. If he hadn't gone to visit Zinn the day before and run late coming back, he might be underneath that tarp right now, with all the other stiffs—or rotting in the desert somewhere, vultures picking at his flesh. So he was lucky in a twisted sort of way.

It hurt to lose the woman, made Stone wish that he had killed her in the States, or when he first crossed into Mexico, instead of keeping her alive. There was no point in brooding on it now, of course, and he would keep his fingers crossed that Tracy might have run her down before he met his end. Whatever, even if she reached the *federales*, Zinn still had the fix in—or he claimed he did, at any rate—and Stone wouldn't be waiting for them when the Mexican police showed up to search the camp. He wouldn't make it easy on his enemies.

Whatever anybody wanted from Chris Stone, from that point onward, they would have to take by force.

His cleanup at the compound would be rudimentary: load any weapons they could salvage into the remaining vehicles, then torch the shacks and bodies. Let them burn, and if the *federales* felt like poking through the ashes, trying to identify a bunch of skeletons from nonexistent dental records, he would wish them luck.

All bad.

Stone's thoughts were focused on survival now, and it was time to move. Someone had clearly followed him from the United States, someone who knew about the woman and wanted her enough to pull this shit and take her back. That meant it wasn't finished yet, and he would have to take decisive steps to save himself.

No problem.

Chris Stone had been taking such decisive steps since boot camp, when he learned to kill and learned that he enjoyed it, that it was a way to keep his pockets filled with spending money. Anyone who tried to take him out was in for a surprise.

A rude awakening, you bet.

Before he put them all to sleep.

"I SAW THIS COMING," Nehemiah Zinn proclaimed, his full beard bristling as if it were alive with static electricity, giving him the aspect of an Old Testament prophet. "I knew this day would be upon us soon."

"Thanks for the tip," Chris Stone replied sarcastically. "It would have been more helpful if I'd known in advance."

Zinn thought about chastising the young man, but then decided not to waste the effort. Stone was rattled, after all, upset by the recent setbacks he had suffered, people chasing after him and all. Zinn knew the feeling well enough, from personal experience. He was a prophet without honor in his own country, driven into the wasteland, just like the Good Book said. His was a small voice crying in the wilderness.

But he would still be heard.

"Some revelations aren't for everyone," he told Stone. "Yahweh speaks to hearts and minds, not right out loud. Some messages he means to share, but others are the private sort—what you'd call need-to-know."

"Uh-huh."

Stone was a skeptic; that was obvious. Zinn didn't care. Faith was a private thing, which he shared with his brethren at the colony. His interest in the Paul Revere Militia was political, an outgrowth of his faith in Yahweh, but distinct and separate from his rites of worship. Faith was of the spirit; war and politics were of the carnal world. It took a wise man to maintain a balance in his life, shortchanging neither worldly honor nor God.

"You're welcome to stay here awhile," Zinn said, "you and your people. We got rules, of course, but nothing complicated. Mind your manners and the Ten Commandments, and I don't see any problem."

"What about the *federales?*" Stone inquired. "They're bound to hear about what happened at the camp last night. It won't be easy to avoid them."

"Won't be necessary to avoid them," Zinn corrected him. "I told you more than once I got the fix in with the Mexican police. They're a backward people, son, but they know all there is about *mordida.*"

"Bribes, you mean," Stone said.

"It's more than that," Zinn explained, speaking as he might have to a backward child, enjoying Stone's apparent irritation. "Down in these parts, it's a way of life. You got to understand how poor this country is before the rest of it falls into place. The paychecks most of these police take home won't feed a healthy sow, much less a family of eight or nine, like most of them raise up down here. The pesos have to come from somewhere, so they do what cops have always done and make it where they can. I grant you that they're not what you or me would call discriminating in their choices, which is why you've got your police all mixed-up in running drugs, assassinations and what-have-you. Still, Yahweh picks his time and place—of that you can be sure. With all that vile corruption going on, it's that much easier for us to buy a little peace of mind while we go on about his work.''

"That's what I said. You pay them off."

Zinn frowned and shook his head. "I'm not real sure I understand your attitude," he said. "You come here asking favors, with your hat in hand, but all the time you're pushing like you're maybe hoping you can piss me off enough to make me turn you down. Why's that?"

Stone waved a hand before his face, as though he were swatting flies. "That wasn't my intention, Nehemiah, really." He was kissing up, now that he thought the door might slam shut in his face, and that was fine. "This whole damn thing has thrown me for a loop, that's all."

"Well, you just take a breather, son," Zinn said. "I don't know what's been going on with you and Pike up north, but I can make a fair guess who was at your boys last night."

Stone blinked at that. "Oh, yeah?"

Zinn smiled with teeth the color of adobe. "Yes, indeed. I wouldn't be at all surprised."

Stone shifted on the simple wooden bench they shared outside Zinn's rectory, the centerpiece—together with his chapel and the well-stocked armory—at Colonia Cristo.

"So, give."

"You ever hear me talk about Emilio Figueras?" Zinn asked.

"It doesn't ring a bell."

"He used to live here at the colony," Zinn said. "Call him my stepson, if you want. His mother was my second wife. Already widowed when I met her, with two growing boys. I preached to her a little, and she saw the light. The boys were saved, too, for a while, but they went bad on me somehow along the way. Emilio first, and then his little brother, Paco."

"They bailed out," Stone offered.

"It was more than just a loss of faith," Zinn replied, refusing to be rushed. "They changed, you understand? Emilio commenced to claiming visions of his own, defying my interpretation of the Scripture. There was nothing for it but to send him packing, and his brother went along. They got their own place now, a few miles south of Rosarito. You can find their mother there, as well, if you're inclined to look for her. She missed the boys too much, I reckon. Blood was more important to her than her soul."

"So you've got competition in the soul-saving department," Stone stated. "I don't see what that's got to do with me."

"You didn't let me finish, son. That attitude again." Zinn let the silence hang between them for a time, then resumed. "The brothers and their people don't just disagree with us here at the colony. They hate us, understand? They hate our friends. We've had some vandalism, scuffles when we've met them accidentally, in town—a shooting not too long ago."

"You're telling me you've got some kind of holy war in progress with a bunch of Mexicans?"

"The struggle between good and evil never ends."

Stone thought about it for a moment and finally shook his head. "It doesn't feel right," he declared. "First off, the raid was carried out by one man, not a group. Another thing, he went directly for my guest. Your wetbacks wouldn't even know she was alive."

"They're only wetbacks when they cross the river," Zinn reminded him. "On this side of the border, we're the foreigners."

"Whatever." Stone was unimpressed.

"The other thing to bear in mind, they're not a stupid people, even if they do sleep through the best part of the afternoon. There are all kinds of ways Emilio and Paco could of heard about your little friend and figured out that snatching her would hit you where it hurts."

"I still don't buy it," Stone replied.

"And I'm not selling anything. I know these boys, is all I'm saying, and they've had a lesson coming to them for a while now. This would be as good a time as any to remind them of their manners, don't you think?"

"Depends on what you have in mind," Stone said.

"A little object lesson. 'He that spareth his rod hateth his son; but he that loveth him chasteneth him betimes.' That's Proverbs 13:24."

"I'll take your word for it."

"Leave everything to me," Zinn told his guest. "You handle it just right, a little chastening goes a long way."

CAPTAIN ROGELIO Rodriguez would have been incensed had anyone described him to his face as lazy or corrupt. He preferred to think of himself as a practical man and a realist, one who had learned certain valuable lessons during his seventeen years with the Mexican Federal Judicial Police. In fact, he tried to learn something each day. It made him feel as if his life had value, and he wasn't merely killing time between the womb and tomb.

One lesson he had mastered early on was that society had no real wish to do away with crime. Some types of crime raised hackles with the rich and powerful, of course: the sort of random rapes and murders that were common in the barrio, plus any kind of theft that jeopardized the holdings of the so-called upper crust. Such incidents were meant to be investigated thoroughly and punished with severity that made the perpetrators an example to their lawless kind. A truly civilized society could never coexist with anarchy.

But at the same time, there were other crimes, defined by statute, that the ruling powers of society preferred to overlook while giving lip service to the eradication of those very acts. White-collar crime, they called it in the States, and many kinds of smuggling fit the bill, as well. In Mexico, as in all other nations, there was an elaborate underground economy that thrived on vice and drugs, embezzlement and fraud, political chicanery, even some corruption in the church. From time to time, that underground economy required housecleaning, blood was spilled, and while such pest control was technically a crime—the crime of murder in the first degree—no one expected the police to break their backs investigating, much less bring anyone to justice.

Once they had raised that rock and started killing all the maggots underneath, where would it end?

Rodriguez walked a fine line in his dealings with the foreigners who looked at Mexico and saw a place of refuge from their native laws, a land they could exploit at bargain rates to further their conspiracies at home. In fact, there was a long tradition of Americans, Canadians and Europeans smuggling contraband through Mexico, investing in illegal enterprises that would turn a hefty profit on the other end. Whenever such men struck a bargain with the powers that be, Rodriguez would receive his orders to cooperate.

And always for a price.

His services weren't tremendously expensive in the scheme of things. It would cost more to smooth the way in Mexicali or the nation's capital than to suborn a captain in the federal police. Every man was known to have his price, and in the system that Rodriguez served, most of those prices were fixed from the top. If he was able to negotiate a better deal on-site, more power to him, but he wouldn't be allowed to gouge the customers unduly, and he had learned not to try.

The gringos at Colonia Cristo and the so-called militia compound outside Rosarito were small-timers in comparison to the Colombians and others who did major business with the government. Essentially they paid for sanctuary and for the official blindness which permitted them to smuggle certain weapons as the spirit moved them. They were big on guns, these strange Americans who hated their own government and yet described themselves as patriots. They spoke of freedom, but Rodriguez sensed that they would readily deny that privilege to many of their fellow citizens if given half a chance. Some of them treated him with thinly veiled contempt, but he was wise enough to pretend he didn't see their sneers.

So far.

The morning summons to Colonia Cristo was unexpected, but Rodriguez took it in stride, drafting three officers to join him and his driver for the short trip from Guerrero Negro. He didn't entirely trust the leader of the colony—a borderline degenerate with crazy eyes who called himself a man of God—but Rodriguez never fully trusted any gringo. It was doubtful that the exiled "patriots" meant any harm, but he made sure his officers were armed with automatic rifles in addition to their side arms, just in case.

The "Reverend" Zinn was waiting for Rodriguez at the compound's outer gate, his beard a bristling rat's nest where the menu of his breakfast was displayed in bits and pieces. Desert sun had baked the gringo's skin until he came close to resembling a native, and his Spanish was acceptable, if burdened with the accent of his native

Oklahoma. They shook hands like lifelong friends, but an observer might have guessed that both men felt a sudden urge to wash their hands.

"You have a problem, Señor Zinn?"

"Unfortunately, yes," Zinn said, and gestured to another man who waited in his shadow, standing back a pace or two. "You've met my good friend, Señor Stone?"

Rodriguez hadn't met him, but he knew the man by reputation, and he almost smiled to see Stone grimace at the mention of his name. Another "patriot" who clearly would have liked to travel incognito.

"I've been looking forward to the pleasure," Rodriguez said as he suffered through another oily handshake. "And how may I be of service?"

"Señor Stone was having dinner here with me last night," Zinn said, "when someone staged a raid on his associates. You know the place, I think?"

"Indeed." Rodriguez cocked an eyebrow, interested despite himself. "Was anybody injured?"

"Several of my men were killed," Stone said in Spanish better than the so-called minister's. "A dozen chased the gunmen when they fled, but none of them returned. I have a party searching for them now, but I assume they've come to harm."

"This is unfortunate," the captain said, "and most unusual. Do you have any notion as to who may be responsible for the attack?"

The gringos glanced at each other, frowning, and it was the bearded man who answered. "We have enemies at home," he said, "too numerous to count. It's why we find ourselves in Mexico today."

One reason, Rodriguez thought, but he kept it to himself. "If you suspect a certain enemy, perhaps you could supply his name."

"It's hard to say," Zinn said. "Still, we're obliged to let

you know about what happened, and we wouldn't want to break the law.''

"The recognition of your civic duty is appreciated," Rodriguez stated, using all his willpower to keep from laughing in the gringo's shaggy face. "I'll drive out to the camp at once, and see if any evidence remains. Of course, you realize there may be nothing useful to be seen."

"That's how it goes sometimes," Zinn said.

"And in the meantime, if you think of anything that might be helpful..."

"You're the first to know."

Another round of handshakes, and the captain turned back toward the car. His officers were waiting for him, two with rifles slung across their shoulders, eyeing several young Americans inside the compound, who were likewise armed as if for war.

A massacre of sorts, Rodriguez thought, but what exactly did it mean? What would the sudden violence in his district mean to him?

A sense of dread rode with the captain as he left the gringo colony behind and started toward the other camp, where death was waiting for him. He could smell it even now, inside the air-conditioned car.

And he imagined that the smell was getting stronger all the time.

THE MORE HE THOUGHT ABOUT the previous night's events, the angrier Chris Stone became. He didn't miss the men who had died; there had been nothing in the way of personal attachment on his part to any of the dead. They meant no more to him than checkers on a game board, strangers for the most part, who had cast their lot with Pike and the militia for whatever reason and had come to grief as a result.

Tough shit.

The woman was another story, not because he cared about her, either, but because she was a threat to him. If she got back alive to the United States, her testimony would be all the government required to charge him with a list of felonies sufficient to ensure that he would spend the last years of his life in prison, looking for parole around the year 2055.

But they would have to catch him first.

He was secure in Mexico—for now, at least—and there was still a chance, however slim, that he could stop the woman cold before she had a chance to sing for her superiors. He had no doubt that she was working for the government—the FBI, or maybe ATF—and he had a strong suspicion that she was connected somehow to the agent Stone had ordered executed back in Idaho some weeks before. If so, and thinking of the way she had behaved with Pike before she tipped her hand and wound up as a prisoner, Stone reckoned there was something like a fifty-fifty chance that she would stick around in Baja for a while and try to bring him down herself.

He hoped so, anyway.

For that would be her last mistake.

Meanwhile, he had to hang around with Zinn and let the *federales* play their games, pretending they expected to discover evidence around his old campsite. There would be none, of course; Stone had already seen to that. If this Rodriguez could make something of the bullet-riddled corpses, he was welcome to them, but Stone wouldn't hold his breath.

Nor was he buying Zinn's wild hare about his rivals, the Figueras brothers. It was foolish to believe that they knew anything about the woman in Stone's camp, or that they would have risked their lives to grab her when she had no relevance to anything in their pathetic peasant lives. Stone didn't need a crystal ball or private message from the Lord to know his enemy had come from the United States, that he was linked somehow to the attack in Idaho and that there would be no escaping him while he was still alive.

So be it.

Stone wasn't by any means averse to killing off his enemies. In fact, he much preferred them dead and buried, where they couldn't bother him again. If Zinn had some old score to settle with the wetbacks who had bailed out of his cult, that was his problem. He would have to settle it himself, without Stone's help.

Right now, Stone faced another problem on his hands, with only one solution, and he dreaded it.

He had to get a message to his contact before the sun went down. He could already hear the man's angry voice, with its accusing tone, before he even broke the latest news.

The sooner he was finished with that part of it, the sooner he could start to track his enemies.

And see them dead.

That pleasure would make all the trouble he had suffered up to now worthwhile.

6

The safehouse in Punta Prieta was rented a year in advance, one of several locations maintained by the DEA agents assigned to drug routes on the Baja peninsula. Bolan had secured a set of keys with Hal Brognola's help and was relieved to find the place available. The furnishings were Spartan, but Ginger Ross took to the two-bedroom house like the Ritz, after her recent captivity in more primitive quarters.

"You get around," she said as Bolan stripped down the Uzi for cleaning.

"I don't like sitting still in any place too long," he said.

"Good thing for me."

"You caught a break," he told her solemnly. "I doubt that it would happen twice."

"Message received. The brass is gunning for me, I suppose."

"I wouldn't know," he told her. "We've got different bosses." Not that Hal Brognola was his boss, exactly, but Bolan didn't plan to brief the lady Fed on Stony Man Farm.

"You told me that in Idaho," she said. "I didn't buy it then, but now I'm wondering."

"Don't waste your energy. If I was ATF, I'd have you on a plane by now, in cuffs if necessary. You'll be lucky if they let you slide with a suspension."

"Lucky? Really?" There was bitterness in Ross's voice. "It doesn't feel like luck. Jeff wasn't lucky."

Bolan knew the pain of losing a partner, someone you had worked with, learned to care for, trusted when your life was riding on the line. He understood but had no time to wallow in a bath of unproductive sympathy.

"There comes a time to cut your losses," he replied.

"I see." An edge of frost had crept into her voice. "So why do you keep coming back?"

"My job's not finished," Bolan said.

She had apparently expected something else, perhaps a statement of concern for her well-being. The woman blinked at his response, sharp color rising in her cheeks, and while her mind was forming a retort, she instantly thought better of it, biting off the words before they passed her lips.

"What *is* your job exactly?"

"I'm dismantling the militia," Bolan said. "So far, they don't think much of the idea."

"I noticed that. You have some kind of license?" Ross asked. "Like a James Bond deal?"

"I don't care much for cloak-and-dagger fiction," Bolan said. "But I could use some information, if you don't mind sharing."

Ross thought about it for a moment, finally nodding. "What the hell," she said. "You've saved my life twice in a week. I guess you've earned a conversation."

It was something anyway. Bolan thought about it for a moment, choosing his words carefully. "What about Baja?" he asked. "I mean, other than the extradition angle, what's the action?"

"Two things I can think of. Are you familiar with the Colony of Christ?" She waited for his nod, then forged ahead. "The guru, Nehemiah Zinn, goes way back in the far-right movement in the States. He was a Klansman for a while, but they weren't tough enough to suit him. Too much talk and not enough action. Around 1979, he formed one of the first militant 'prolife' organizations. Called it USA—that stands for Us Against Abortion—if you can believe it. Seven clinic fires and bombings later, he was wanted on an arson charge, with a side order of conspiracy.

"He wound up going underground, got busted back in '83, and served about two years of a seven-year federal sentence. Apparently, it pushed him over the edge. He had a few more 'revelations' in his cell and came out preaching Armageddon in our time. By now, he was too far gone for most of the religious right, but he found enough disciples to follow him south of the border in early '87. He's been down here ever since, waiting for the Second Coming and making ends meet any way he can, including arms deals with his fellow paranoids back in the States."

"Which explains the ATF interest," Bolan said.

"Bingo. No matter what his psycho buddies say, we couldn't care less how he runs his so-called church—until he breaks the law, that is. Which, in Zinn's case, primarily consists of smuggling ventures, mostly weapons, going back and forth across the border. We're convinced that he's shipped different kinds of bargain-basement military hardware to the California Empire Knights, the SS Battle Korps and half a dozen other fringe groups on the right, all racist, anti-Semite, paramilitary types."

"Arrests?" Bolan asked.

"Small-fry. They do the minimum and keep their mouths shut. That's one thing about a holy war. You get good haters."

"And the Mexican authorities just look the other way?"

"Two things to keep in mind," she said. "The first one is *mordida*—the endemic bribery that makes the wheels go 'round in Mexico. If you find anyone in government who isn't on the take somehow, I want his name and address. It's expected here, like some kind of unofficial overtime program."

"The other thing?" he prompted her.

"The whole religious angle. I don't know if you read about the so-called Lambs of God a few years back, but they were one of several dozen cults that started out in the United States and moved to set up shop in northern Mexico. Nice weather, lower prices—and the law will basically let you do anything you want, for a price. Right now you've got polygamists, free-love cults, flying-saucer worshipers and several groups like Zinn's, who have their politics and their religion mixed so thoroughly you can't tell them apart."

"No problems, eh?"

"Well, not from the police," she said. "A while back, we know there was a major rift in Nehemiah's congregation. Several dissidents walked out and started their own colony a few miles up the road. Since then, there's been a lot of tension in the neighborhood, folks waiting for the other shoe to drop."

Bolan thought that might be worth a look, but his mind had already moved on. "You mentioned weapons going back and forth across the border," he remarked.

"Oh, sure, the traffic goes both ways. In the States, some of your hard-core nuts want military weapons on the cheap. In Mexico, sometimes it's just the other way around. Are you familiar with the Zapatista movement?"

"Yes." He had to keep from smiling at the question, for he knew the rebel movement inside out. Most of its members were mestizos, descendants of ancient Mayan stock, who had taken up arms against alleged oppression of their people by the Mexican government. The civil war had sputtered on for years, with periods of vicious fighting interrupted by negotiations that restored uneasy peace, but only for brief intervals.

"Well, there you go. We have information that the Paul Revere Militia has been using Zinn and others like him to move stolen guns across the border, sell them to guerrillas and then use the cash back home to finance their campaign against the 'Jewish government' in the United States.''

"The Zapatistas are considered leftists," Bolan said. "That shouldn't go down well with men like Pike and Zinn."

"That's true enough, but then again, their money's green. Also you've got the notion of a grass-roots native army standing up against a government that's viewed, by most of the far right, as a lapdog of the liberals in Washington. In the end, their actual beliefs and principles are less important than the image they project. You follow me? It's like the Klan boys rubbing shoulders with Black Muslims in the sixties. Even though they hate each other, they have certain common goals."

"There's lots of ground to cover," Bolan said.

"I grant you, I could use some help."

He finally smiled at that, and shook his head. "You're wanted elsewhere," he informed her. "Urgently, at that. Besides, you don't have jurisdiction."

"And you do?"

"Call it the rule of hot pursuit," he said. "I try to cut through the red tape."

"I noticed that. It's nice work if you can get it."

"That depends on how you handle it."

"You seem to do all right," she said.

"That's me," he told her pointedly.

"So, I could use a second chance."

"I don't have time to cover you." As Bolan spoke, his hands were reassembling the Uzi SMG. "Besides, you're on a personal vendetta, and your targets are back in the States."

"Except for Stone."

"Leave him to me."

"Is that an order?"

"Take it any way you want."

She stared at Bolan for a moment, while the silence stretched between them, and a frown tugged at the corners of her mouth. "We'll see," she said at last. "We'll see."

"WE MUST BE STEADFAST in the hour of tribulation and prepared to meet our enemies!" Zinn's thick beard moved in time with his lips as he spoke, resembling an animated thornbush. "If we falter, we are lost! Our cause is lost! Our very souls are lost!"

A scattered handful of his audience responded with "Amens," although it seemed to Zinn that they lacked real conviction. If the spirit of the Lord were truly in them, he would have them on their feet by now.

Try harder.

"You all know the vipers who would love to see us cut and run," he said. "Give up all that we've worked for through the years, admit defeat and run away like whipped dogs in the night. We know their names, by God! Who are they?"

No one answered him, and Zinn experienced a moment of disorientation as he stared back at his flock. Sometimes—increasingly, of late—he wondered whether he was wasting his time on a bunch of idiots who followed him because they needed someone, *anyone,* to tell them what to think. Zinn didn't like to think about that possibility, because it made him doubt his calling, and if he hadn't been called by Yahweh to pursue this fight, then who or what was he?

"Their names!" he bellowed. "Don't be shy, for God's sake! Name our enemies!"

"Figueras?" someone called out from the cheap seats toward the back.

"Yes, brother! There's a man who knows his Scripture. 'O generation of vipers, who hath warned you to flee from the wrath to come?' Matthew 3:7, that is. And our wrath is coming, brethren. Let the vipers heed my warning if they will. 'None is so fierce that dare stir him up: who then is able to stand before me?' Job 41:10.''

"Amen!'' came back at him a little stronger then, from roughly two-thirds of the audience.

"Yahweh has told us to prepare ourselves for battle, brethren, and we've done as he commands. We have the wherewithal to grind our enemies beneath our heels, but do we have the will?''

No one replied to that, and Zinn plunged on before the sudden stillness could embarrass him, infect his people with a spirit of timidity.

"The enemy is at our very gates!'' he shouted, pointing out across their heads, disgusted when a couple of them turned and glanced back at the tall doors of the chapel, as if they expected the Figueras brothers to be standing there. Dumb bastards.

"We must face him like the godly soldiers we pretend to be!'' Zinn ranted on, feeling them warm to his cause the longer he spoke. Sometimes he railed at them for hours on end, unloading every bit of anger and frustration he could dredge up from his weary soul. They seemed to eat it up.

"Yes, Lord!'' a gaunt-faced woman cried out from the second row. Of course, she wouldn't be sent out to fight. She could afford enthusiasm.

"It is time for us to wipe out this great pestilence that has already plagued us for too long! 'I beseech you therefore, brethren, by the mercies of God, that ye present your bodies a living sacrifice, holy, acceptable unto God, which is your reasonable service.' Romans 12:1. Is there any here among you who would fail our Father in his hour of need?''

No hands went up, which had to be a good sign, anyway. "Who volunteers to help me rid the earth of these vile infidels?'' Zinn asked the crowd, and smiled as hands began to levitate. He had them now. "God bless you, breth-ren, but we only need the men for this mission. Those of you between the ages of, let's say eighteen and forty, if you'd stay awhile, the rest may be excused with blessings from our Lord. Go on, now. Tend to business! Say your prayers!"

Zinn waited while the women, children and a handful of the older men filed out, the latter leaving with reluctance, since they smelled a fight. The exodus left close to thirty men behind, all watching him and waiting for their orders, the expressions on their faces offering a fair reflection of respective zeal.

"All right," he said at last, bent forward with his fore-arms resting on the podium, for all the world resembling a bearded praying mantis. "Here's what I want you to do...."

STONE DREADED the telephone call, but there was no way around it. His sponsor had to be informed of what had happened. He would find out anyway—Stone knew that from experience, the one time he had tried to hold a bit of bad news back—and it would only make things worse if he was forced to ask about it.

The worst part would be the cumulative picture. First, he had been driven out of Idaho, then out of the States and now his unknown enemies were hounding him in Baja. They—or he, as the survivors of the latest raid still dog-gedly insisted there had been only one man involved—had stolen his hole card, wiped out at least half of his troops on-site, rendered the compound uninhabitable, driving him to seek refuge with Nehemiah Zinn and his demented cultoids. None of that would go down well with his em-ployer. There was no damn reason why it should.

One thing about professionals: when they paid money—and lots of it—for a certain job to be performed, they ex-pected results. Chris Stone had done all right for his employer until recently, the past two weeks or so, when it began to fall apart. It would be helpful if he could ascribe his latest failures to some grand conspiracy against him, but his failure to identify and neutralize the enemy would still weigh heavily against him in his sponsor's mind.

Enough delays.

The town of Rosarito boasted two motels, both run-down tourist traps that overcharged for tiny rooms with bargain-basement furniture and tap water that nearly guaranteed unwary drinkers a case of Montezuma's revenge. Stone didn't plan to spend the night or drink the water, though. He needed a telephone jack, which Zinn couldn't provide him at his colony, and this had been the quickest access he could find.

The telephone he plugged into the wall was a speciality number, carrying a built-in scrambler and a switch that let him change the pitch and tenor of his voice at will. He could become a woman if he wanted to, or sing bass for the Mormon Tabernacle Choir, but that wouldn't be necessary with the scrambler engaged. He doubted whether anyone was tapped into the sponsor's telephone or tracing his incoming calls—the man had always seemed too smart for that—but you could never be too safe, especially when unknown enemies were breathing down your neck.

He made the call and waited until a soft, familiar voice came on the line. The number told him that his man was still in the United States, more than a thousand miles away, but from the sound of him, he could have been next door.

"Hello." Unlike most people, this person didn't pose his greeting as a question.

"It's me," Stone said, regretting it at once. The man knew who it was. He had an ear for voices, probably a caller-ID box gave Stone's number, or at least the general area that he was calling from.

"You've had another problem."

No, he wasn't psychic, though he almost seemed that way at times. Stone's scheduled check-in was almost six hours late, and that spelled trouble in itself.

"That's right," he said. "You're scrambling?"

"Certainly."

It was another stupid question, wasted breath. The bastard made him feel inadequate sometimes, the only person Stone knew personally who could do that. Part of it was knowing that the man could reach out anytime he wanted to and crush him like an insect, but the rest came from the way he operated, covering the moves before an adversary thought of them, much less began to execute a plan. He had one of those steel-trap minds, and that was always dangerous.

"Somebody hit the camp last night," Stone said, his hand white knuckled where he gripped the telephone. "I lost an estimated twenty men. Also the woman."

"Dead?"

Stone didn't have to ask whom his employer meant. Cold-hearted player that he was, he cared no more about Stone's soldiers than the mercenary did himself. They were game pieces, tools to use until they broke or lost their edge, at which point they were simply thrown away. The woman, likewise, was no big deal in and of herself. His sponsor wasn't worried that she might be injured. Rather, he was looking for some reassurance that she wouldn't be around to file a formal charge or testify in court.

"Escaped," Stone told him bluntly. "Rescued, I should say. From what I hear, she was the focus of the raid."

"From what you hear?" The voice had taken on a cutting edge.

"I wasn't at the compound when the raid went down. I had some business over at the colony, you know?"

"How very fortunate."

Stone felt the angry color heating up his face. He felt

like screaming curses, maybe slamming down the telephone, but he couldn't afford a temper tantrum. Not today, of all days.

"I'm on top of it," he said, hating himself not for the lie, but for the failure it was calculated to conceal. "I'll make it right."

"I hope so, Christopher."

"Hey, if you don't think I can pull it off—"

"It's just a trifle late to look for a replacement, don't you think?"

Again Stone swallowed the reply that came to mind, and he said, "I'm taking care of it. You have my word."

"In that case—" the hesitation was long enough to make him sweat "—we have no problem, do we?"

"No. No, we don't."

"I'm glad to hear it, Christopher. I was...concerned."

"You can relax," Stone said, and nearly laughed aloud at his own words. The only way this bastard would relax was in his coffin, and the odds were fifty-fifty that he would be ready with a lethal comeback even then.

"I will," his sponsor told him, which was a transparent lie.

"Okay. Unless I have some news, let's say this time again, the day after tomorrow."

"Christopher." The calm voice stopped him. "I hope you have some news." And then the link was broken, just like that.

Again Stone fought the urge to vent his anger and frustration on the telephone receiver in his hand. It would have been a waste of effort, though. He needed that aggression to defeat his enemies. They had already run him ragged, cut him off at every turn the past few days, but he wasn't surrendering. It wasn't in his nature to give up. There was a list Stone carried in his head, the names of men who had learned that lesson the hard way and paid for the instruction with their lives.

Stone didn't need his sponsor's urging to take care of business, to defend himself, but it provided fresh incentive, knowing that he couldn't simply disengage, lie low, return to fight another day. He had a schedule, was committed to the sponsor's master plan, and if he blew it...well, the world would be a small, unfriendly place.

It had to be done right, then, Stone decided, starting with the bastards who pursued him.

Starting now.

AFIF ABDUL RAHMAN WASN'T prepared to worry yet. He was concerned about the timetable, of course, the possibility that Stone might fail, but there were worse things that could happen. All that really mattered in the long run—what Americans would call the bottom line—was that his name and link to Hezbollah, his role in the jihad, shouldn't be publicized. Aside from that imperative, his plans were flexible in the extreme, no matter what he told Christopher Stone.

The plan had been Rahman's brainchild. He had been watching CNN in Baghdad, resting up after a mission to Algeria, when he had seen a spot on the militia movement in America. It was big news, apparently, these bands of men who armed themselves and posed as "freedom fighters," claiming that their government was run by Communists and Jews. Rahman wasn't prepared to argue that point with them; rather, he had seen potential in the movement, opportunity for someone to step in, provide a guiding hand, direct the "patriots" and counsel them as to the form their holy war should take.

Most of them feared or hated Jews already, which was half the battle. He wasn't concerned about their hatred for the blacks, Latinos, Asians or homosexuals. *Focus* was the key to any handler's ultimate success. It didn't matter if the pawn's attention wandered, just as long as there was someone standing by to bring him back on track.

The single, glaring flaw in Rahman's plan was that American militiamen would look at any Arab with the same contempt they felt for immigrants, nonwhites and "liberated" females. He would need a front man, someone they could trust, admire, aspire to emulate, a warrior who embodied all that the militias were supposed to stand for—but a hero with a price tag, all the same.

Christopher Stone had been his final choice, selected from a field of thirteen candidates. The other twelve had long since disappeared, four after turning down Rahman's offer, the other nine by simple process of elimination, once he chose his man. Hell had no fury like a mercenary scorned, and there was no room for a leak in Rahman's master plan. Anyone not beholden to him was an enemy.

The rest of it was relatively simple. Once Stone chose a group and infiltrated, worked his way up to command rank in the private army of his choice, he would direct the "soldiers" into ever more aggressive and disruptive actions, spreading fear in the United States, increasing personal antipathy to Washington by any means available, provoking passage of new antiterrorism legislation that would ultimately backfire on the U.S. government as the excesses of the FBI and CIA had done back in the 1970s. They had devised a timetable of incidents, including robberies, assassinations, bombings, but it made little difference in the long run if specific acts were carried out on schedule—or at all, for that matter. What mattered to Afif Rahman, and to his masters, was the ultimate effect of terrorism from within, apparently directed by Americans against Americans.

The rest of it, as Rahman's enemies would say, was simply frosting on the cake.

He was concerned about Stone's fate today because of what the man might do or say if he was forced into a corner, offered something in the nature of a trade to save his life. The same end might result, of course, if Stone thought Rahman had abandoned him. The mercenary had to know he was expendable—that was a fact of life in his profession, after all—but it wouldn't do for him to discover that Rahman had planned to sacrifice him from day one of their association. That alone might prompt him to defect, jump ship, tell all he knew to the authorities.

But not just yet.

Rahman considered himself a fair judge of character, and he believed Stone would need a greater impetus than any of his recent setbacks to betray his handler. He was being well paid for a service that, until the past few days, had involved little personal risk. Now that the time had come to earn his danger money, pride and greed would keep him on the firing line.

For now, at least.

And when the time came to dispose of him, when he could no longer be trusted, Rahman knew exactly what to do.

He was an expert at disposal, a professional who enjoyed his work.

7

The dune buggies were perfect. They had been an inspiration from Lord Yahweh. Pastor Zinn had said so when he ordered their construction, and while Randy Burke had harbored certain doubts in the beginning, he could see now that the prophet was correct.

As always.

How else could you really tell a holy man apart from all the fakers if it wasn't by their knowledge and their deeds? There was a Bible verse that said, "Ye know the man and his communication." Burke couldn't give the right citation at the moment, with his mind preoccupied the way it was, but he still got the message loud and clear. Zinn was one great holy man—perhaps *the* holy man. The very thought of it made Burke feel humble, and he had to put it out of mind.

Because he didn't need a humble spirit at the moment. What he needed was an eye for war, a taste for blood. The prophet had selected him to lead this mission, and he wouldn't tolerate the thought of failure.

The last two miles had been difficult, since they were forced to push the buggies, rolling with the lights and engines off, to keep from waking up anybody in the Figueras camp. Colonia Verdad, they called it—Colony of Truth—as if to add insult on top of injury. It wasn't bad enough that the Figueras brothers—damn their souls to everlasting hell!—had seen fit to defect from Zinn and lead a handful of their friends and relatives into the outer darkness. That kind of thing went on with churches all the time back in the States. When they set up their own religious commune, just a few miles down the road from Colonia Cristo, that would have been enough to set some pastors off, but Zinn was made of stronger stuff. He let them be and gave them all the rope they needed, just to hang themselves with lies.

The last straw, though, was when Emilio Figueras started preaching to his flock that Pastor Zinn wasn't a man of God at all, but something closer to a gringo Antichrist. That kind of blasphemy demanded retribution, and when coupled with the bold attack on the militia compound not far from Colonia Cristo, it was a clear-cut signal that the heretics from Colonia Verdad were looking for an all-out war.

This night, they were about to see their wish come true. And Randy Burke had been assigned to make it happen. What an honor! What rewards would be stored up for him in heaven, whether he survived this night or not!

Of course, Plan A had Burke coming out on top, victorious, returning to Colonia Cristo for a hero's welcome.

Each of the dune buggies was built for two, a driver up in front, with a machine gunner who sat behind and slightly to his left. The guns were Browning .30-calibers, the air-cooled models that were used in World War II and later in Korea. They were old but well maintained, still deadly at a hundred yards, and for this night's work, you could cut that range by half, at least. Each buggy had 2,000 rounds of ammunition, plus the Ruger Mini-14 rifles, side arms and grenades each passenger was carrying. Five buggies, and another ten men who had come by truck and walked the last two miles, helped push the main attack vehicles over sand and rocky ground. It was a twenty-man assault force for a colony of forty-five or fifty souls, half of them kids and women.

It would have to be enough.

Burke palmed his plastic walkie-talkie, thumbed down the red transmitter button, and whispered to the microphone, "Heads up! It's time!"

There was a burst of static as he let the button go, and a disgruntled-sounding voice came back at him. "Say what?"

Another chimed in on the heels of that one, saying, "Speak up, will you!"

Red-faced with embarrassment, Burke tried again, speaking louder this time, swallowing his fear that someone in the target camp would hear him. What good would it do them if they did?

"Heads up!" he snarled into the compact two-way radio. "It's time! We roll on three, my count!"

The voices that came back to him this time were all acknowledging his order. Burke noted four of them and started to count.

On "One," as prearranged, the engines roared to life, letting the Figueras brothers and their people know they were surrounded and about to feel the wrath of God.

On "Two," the headlights blazed, high beams, like vengeful dragons' eyes that lit up every corner of the coming battle zone, leaving the infidels nowhere to hide.

On "Three," the buggies started forward, fat tires spewing sand behind them, and the charge was on.

Burke kept a firm grip on his Browning .30-caliber machine gun and prayed that he had what it took to be a Christian hero for his people, even when he faced a trial by fire.

EMILIO FIGUERAS HEARD the demons coming. He had been expecting them for weeks—in fact, since he and Paco found the courage to abandon Pastor Zinn's domain of lies—but passing time had almost lulled him into thinking they were safe.

Almost.

It hadn't stopped him from collecting weapons when and where he could, or teaching his disciples how to use them properly. The residents of Colonia Verdad weren't warriors, but they would defend themselves and fight to the death, if need be, for their wives and children.

Emilio was only hoping that it wouldn't come to that.

The engine sounds of the advancing dune buggies almost drowned out the warning cries from sentries he had posted at the corners of the camp in wooden guard towers. They should have seen the hit team coming, but there was no moon, and shadows in the desert could play tricks with even the most cautious eyes. There had been no headlights or engine noise before the sudden glare and blast of sound that told Emilio his compound was surrounded.

"To the walls!" he shouted, trusting all his disciples to recall their dress rehearsals for a day—or night—like this one, when the enemy would strike.

In fact, the walls were more like split-rail fences, with some barbed wire interwoven through the gaps. They offered no real cover from a bullet, and they wouldn't stop a speeding car or truck, although Emilio hoped they might be strong enough to snag a lightweight dune buggy.

The sharp, staccato sound of automatic weapons made him duck his head as he was running toward his post. Crimson tracers flew across the compound, crossing paths like fireflies in some kind of mating frenzy, acting out the rites of spring. In fact, this was a feeding frenzy, angry blood flies swarming, seeking prey. Emilio saw the tracers coming for him, arcing through the night, and hit the dirt before they got there, listened to them snapping overhead, mere inches from his face.

His weapon was an M-1 carbine with a 30-round banana clip. It didn't have much stopping power at great distances, but that should be no problem, since his enemies apparently intended to destroy him in his own backyard.

As Emilio scrambled to his feet once more, his soldiers in the watchtowers were firing two vintage Browning automatic rifles and a pair of M-16s. Most of the other weapons in the camp were rifles, shotguns, pistols and two ancient Thompson submachine guns that Emilio had purchased from some teenage gangsters in Tijuana months before. He had some dynamite laid by, as well, but it wasn't designed as a defensive weapon, to be used in one's own home.

He heard a loud crack as one of the dune buggies struck a fence off to his right some forty yards away. The fence held for a moment, several of his people running off in that direction, braving fire from the machine gun mounted on the dune buggy, but it couldn't withstand a second blow. He saw the vehicle burst through, balloon tires jolting over fallen timbers, barbed-wire streamers trailing from its skeletal body. The gunner still fired his weapon, dropping his selected targets with short precision bursts.

Emilio cursed, taking the Lord's name in vain, a pang of guilt stabbing into his chest even as he raised the M-1 carbine to his shoulder. Repentance would have to wait, he decided, peering through the carbine's open sights to find his moving target. And if something happened to him, if he died in sin, then he would have to throw himself upon God's mercy, make him understand that he was caught up in a mortal conflict with the spawn of Satan. Grappling with the hosts of evil was a trial for anyone; even Christ had lost his temper now and then.

Emilio squeezed off three rounds toward the dune buggy, uncertain if he scored with any of his shots, and was about to follow after it on foot when discipline kicked in. It would have meant abandoning his post, his personal responsibility,

and flying in the face of everything that he had tried to
teach his followers.

He would maintain his post, which had been drawn by
lot, and do the best he could against the enemies who found
him there. Some instinct told him there would shortly be
enough of them to go around.

BOLAN WAS WATCHING as the strike team rolled into position, taking up their posts, communicating by means of
hand signs and muffled walkie-talkies. He could probably
have intervened to throw them off their schedule, but it
would have been a hasty effort, no more than a stop-gap
measure, and he owed the targets nothing, as it was. They
were another group of gun-toting religious zealots who, if
Ginger Ross had judged them accurately, broke with Nehemiah Zinn on issues that owed more to private egos than
interpretation of the Scriptures.

Cults were like that, always breaking up, regrouping,
new "messiahs" trying to cash in on gullible disciples
when and where they could. Increasingly such groups were
prone to violence, and not only in the Third World precincts
where such mayhem was expected. Back in the United
States, the jails and morgues were filling up with self-styled
swamis, Hare Krishnas, half-baked Satanists and Christian
"patriots" who tried to place themselves and their desires
above the law.

When Bolan heard the engines rev and saw the headlights blaze to life, he was confronted with a choice. He
could sit back and watch the show, perhaps mop up the
winners, or he could pursue a variation of the plan that
brought him to Colonia Verdad—which was to speak with
Zinn's religious opposition and attempt to put a new twist
on the Baja blitz. If nothing else, there was a decent chance
that they had information even Ginger Ross didn't possess,
concerning Zinn and the militia's dealings with the Zapa-

tista rebels, their connections to the government, perhaps their source of arms.

The shooting made his mind up for him, as .30-caliber machine guns sprayed death and tracers through the camp from five directions as the dune buggies closed in. He also spotted scattered infantry, though it appeared that there were fewer than a dozen foot soldiers involved. However much Zinn hated the defectors from his cult, he clearly wouldn't risk his whole force on a massed attack.

Bolan went down to join them, going in behind the raiders. He was dressed in black, his face darkened, carrying the Uzi with its suppressor in place, to make himself a trifle less obtrusive in the general din of battle. There was still a chance some sentry might get lucky, drop him on the run, but he would have to take that risk or let the game play on without him while he lingered on the sidelines.

Not this time.

He found himself beneath one of the guard towers, the gunner up above him firing at the nearest dune buggy with something heavy. Spent casings pattered on the sand near Bolan's feet, but he wasn't distracted as the buggy turned back toward the tower, moving on a hard collision course. Its gunner had his Browning MG cranked back on his mount, the barrel elevated skyward, as he fired short bursts at the defender in the tower. Bolan heard his bullets striking wood, then a strangled cry of pain, immediately followed by another short burst from the heavy automatic rifle.

Bolan chose that moment to unleash a burst of parabellum shockers from his Uzi, aiming from the shoulder, stitching holes across the driver's chest and slamming him against his padded seat. The dune buggy began to swerve, its gunner rocking, losing aim, and the Executioner had him cold before he could recover, much less leave his seat to grab the steering wheel. A second burst, and the machine gunner was airborne, no seat belt to hold him as he vaulted from the buggy and the skeletal machine rolled on without him, running with a dead man at the wheel.

The tower sentry chased it with another long burst from his automatic rifle, perhaps believing he had scored some kind of luck hit and saved the day. But if it puzzled him at all, he didn't hesitate to find another target, emptying the rifle's magazine in seconds flat and pausing to reload.

Bolan would never have a better chance to move, and so he took it, breaking from the cover of the tower's shadow, running toward the clustered buildings that made up the heart of the Figueras compound. Any resident who met him would assume he was the enemy and act accordingly, in which case Bolan had no qualms about reacting to defend himself. He would prefer to let them live for now, however, and address the common enemy, but it would take finesse to pull it off.

And sometimes, in the middle of a firefight, pure finesse was hard to find.

THE WORMS HAD MORE FIGHT in them than he had imagined, but the victory would still belong to Randy Burke if he had anything to say about it. Even as the thought took shape, a couple of Colonia Verdad's people ran into the buggy's glaring headlights, and he cut them down without a second thought, the .30-caliber projectiles shredding flesh and fabric as they jittered, twisted and sprawled like dirty rag dolls on the ground.

This night wasn't the first time Burke had killed a man. He had been wanted in the States for robbery and murder when he made his way to Baja, stumbled into Pastor Zinn by accident and thereby found Lord Yahweh waiting to receive him. In his other life, however, killing had been part of business, nothing he was proud of for its own sake, even when he bragged about it to his cronies in the joint.

But this was different. Killing for the prophet—for the

Lord—made Burke feel powerful. He was a righteous Christian soldier, fighting on the side of God Almighty, and his truth was marching on. Colonia Verdad, for all intents and purposes, was history.

Another running figure dodged across his headlights, but he saw a flash of blue—the arm bands they had chosen to distinguish one another from their enemies—and held his fire. A heartbeat later, close behind his soldier, came another enemy defender. The runner spun to face him, blinking in the headlights' glare, and tried to raise his rifle, but the reflex came too late. A stream of bullets ripped into his chest and slammed him over backward, sprawling on his butt before the buggy plowed him under, bouncing heavily across his corpse.

Good riddance.

A bullet spanged into the left rear fender of the buggy, bringing Burke around to face another enemy. He had to leave his seat to pivot the machine gun far enough, but he was well braced in the vehicle, with no risk of falling out unless they rolled.

"Hard left!" he told his driver, shouting to be heard above the roar of gunfire as he cut loose with the .30-caliber again. The wheelman did as he was told, but dune buggies required deft handling, and they didn't turn on a dime. The roll bar would protect his driver if they spilled, but Burke had left his safety belt unfastened for this very reason, to prevent himself from being open, helpless, to an adversary on his flank.

He saw not one, but two assailants breaking for the cover of a Quonset hut as he maneuvered to retaliate for their unmanly—and incompetent—surprise attack. The Browning stuttered, bright flame lancing from its muzzle, tracers shimmering like windblown sparks in hot pursuit of Burke's moving targets. One of them was almost to the hut when the bullets found him. Half a dozen rounds tore through his upper back and shoulders, while a tracer set his shaggy hair on fire.

The other gunman, running second, saw his partner die and tried to veer around the falling body without breaking stride, but it was still enough to throw him off his pace. A slight job with the Browning's muzzle, swinging to the right, and he was spinning like a figure skater, but without the flashy costume or the sense of style. The buggy's right front fender caught him as he fell and slammed him backward, sprawling facedown in the sand.

Away to Burke's left, near the center of the compound, an explosion rocked the night. He didn't know if one of his men was responsible, and he didn't care. Destruction of the camp was his assignment, and it made no difference if the heretics helped out by blowing up their own supplies and dwellings. It would even be poetic justice in a way, the kind of thing that would make Pastor Zinn rejoice with glee.

He glanced in the direction of the blast, saw leaping flames and one of his dune buggies lying on its side. The driver's seat was empty, but a body sprawled behind the vehicle, and Burke could see the bright blue arm band, flecked with blood now, even through a pall of drifting smoke.

"Get over there!" Burke told his driver, pointing through the haze toward the capsized buggy. With a nod, the driver swung their vehicle hard left, maneuvering around a body sprawled in his path, and stood on the accelerator.

Burke had been counting on a rapid victory—a massacre, in fact—but it was turning out to be a more prolonged fight than he had expected. He had obviously suffered losses, and there might be more, but he was still convinced that victory lay well within his grasp. The first advantage of surprise was bolstered by superior weapons and training, not to mention the strong right arm of the Lord.

With him, all things were possible. Some simply required more effort than others. More sweat. More tears.

More blood.

THE GUNNER ON THE SECOND dune buggy almost got lucky. Firing from a range of thirty yards or so, from Bolan's blind side, he came close enough that the warrior felt the .30-caliber projectiles snapping past him, flying faster than the speed of sound. In one smooth motion, Bolan swung around to face his enemy and hit the deck, thereby depriving his assailant of a target.

The dune buggy's driver had his vehicle aimed straight at Bolan, the engine revving loudly as he charged. Supported on his elbows, the Executioner aimed the Uzi, squeezing off three short bursts in succession, parabellum bullets ripping into both front tires before they found the buggy's driver, and took his head off at the eyebrows. The vehicle began to swerve, then the brakes locked with a dead foot on the pedal, flipping it as if it were a toy.

As with the gunner in the first vehicle he had taken out, this one had chosen to forego his seat belt, trusting luck to keep him in his seat. He couldn't manage to defy the laws of physics, though, and he was flung clear of the buggy as it rolled, a fledgling acrobat who vaulted through the smoky air and landed heavily, without a hint of grace. Unquestionably injured, still the gunner struggled to his feet and tried to orient himself, his right hand groping for the pistol on his hip.

He never made it.

Bolan shot him in the chest from forty feet away, a 3-round burst that struck with all the impact of a hammer blow and punched his target backward. The shooter's heels drummed briefly on the sandy soil, arms flailing like a dreamer mimicking the backstroke in his sleep, before he finally lay still.

Two more for Bolan, but he wasn't finished yet. Around him, as he scrambled to his feet, the battle raged. Three dune buggies were still in action, plus a number of the foot soldiers who had come in behind them, readily identifiable by the blue arm bands they wore over camouflage fatigues.

As Bolan went in search of other targets, he could see why Baja held so much allure for rejects and escapees from polite society. Competing settlements were few and far between, policemen rarer still. The present battle might go on all night, if able-bodied men and ammunition lasted long enough, with no complaints from nosy neighbors, no embarrassing reports to the authorities.

The Baja landscape was a desert, for the most part, but it was a place where jungle law prevailed: survival of the fittest, kill or be killed, tooth and claw—or, in this case, gun and grenade.

Right now, it could go either way, and while he had no abstract reason to support the camp's defenders, Bolan still believed they could be useful to his cause.

But only if they were alive.

Determined to prevent their slaughter if he could, the Executioner moved on in search of human prey.

8

Emilio Figueras huddled near the window of a bullet-riddled Quonset hut and waited for his life to flash before his eyes. It was supposed to happen at the point of death, he understood, and every passing moment made it seem less likely that he would survive the raid by Nehemiah Zinn's commandos. Better than a dozen of his followers were dead already, and while he had seen one of the attacking dune buggies disabled, the remainder were still racing through the camp, spraying the buildings and his people with machine-gun fire. On top of that, there were foot soldiers from the other side, as well, distinguishable in the firelit night by sky-blue arm bands that reminded him, ironically, of the apparel favored by United Nations peace-keepers.

Emilio knew the irony was unintentional. Whatever Zinn might be—a bigot, charlatan or raving madman—he wasn't a subtle humorist. Most likely, there had been some spare cloth at his compound, maybe remnants from the ladies' sewing circle, and the prophet had appropriated it to dress up his soldiers for war.

His mind was wandering, Emilio realized as he was snapped back to the present by the sound of an explosion and the sting of perspiration in his eyes. Most nights were chilly in the Baja desert, even when the daytime temperatures topped 110 degrees, but he was sweating from exertion.

And fear.

If he were honest with himself, Emilio Figueras would admit that he was terrified. His faith in God Almighty was as strong as any man's, but it had also brought him to his present circumstance, and he was well aware that God helped those who helped themselves. Napoleon had phrased it differently, suggesting that God favored those with large battalions on the battlefield, and while Emilio's disciples physically outnumbered Zinn's strike team, they hadn't spent the time on paramilitary training that would make the crucial difference in a firefight.

It was his fault, he allowed, too late.

A couple of Zinn's foot soldiers appeared, advancing on the hut where he had gone to ground. Emilio saw them from his window, edging back another pace to take advantage of the darkness as he raised his M-1 carbine, braced the wooden stock against his shoulder, squinting as he aimed. As far as he could tell, the gunmen weren't wearing body armor. If he took his time and did it properly…

His first shot struck the pointman just off center, in the chest, and staggered him. The wounded soldier didn't fall immediately, but he clasped one hand against his chest, blood spilling through his fingers as he lurched to one side.

The second gunman saw his partner hit, but didn't recognize the source of fire in time to save himself. Emboldened by his first success, Emilio squeezed off three more rounds in rapid fire and watched the target slump back on his haunches with a dazed expression on his face. When he collapsed, the first man was still on his feet, resisting the inevitable, so Emilio shot him twice more in the face and put him down.

Encouraged by that small success, Emilio rose and edged his way toward the door of the hut, still fearful of exposure to the enemy, but knowing that he had nowhere to hide. The carbine in his hands felt vastly heavier than its six pounds, but he clung fast, as if his life depended on the weapon—which, in fact, it did.

Another loud explosion echoed through the compound, and he wondered once again if the attacking force was using hand grenades or if his people were resorting to the stock of aging dynamite they kept on hand. Emilio knew that there was only one way to find out, and he would never do it hiding in the darkness while his followers were fighting for their lives.

It was his fault that they were here and facing death from Zinn's commandos.

He reached the open doorway, peered around the corner for a moment, smelling gun smoke in the air, then stepped outside.

If death was waiting for him, he would meet it like a man.

THE RAID HAD STARTED off all right, as far as Randy Burke could tell, but it had hit some kind of unexpected snag during the past few minutes, and he had already lost two dune buggies, together with their crews. If that kept up—well, it had damn well better not keep up, or he was in deep shit.

He was lining up a clear shot at a huddled group of targets when he noticed that he had used up his first full belt of ammunition for the Browning. Cursing and apologizing to the Lord all at once, Burke disengaged the empty box and shouted for his driver to slow down a minute. He grabbed another box and opened it, attached it to the weapon, lifted out the free end of the belt and fed it into the receiver. When the piece was primed and ready, he glanced up and saw his targets vanishing around the corner of a storage shed.

"Get after them!" Burke ordered.

"Gotcha!" the wheelman barked. He stood on the accelerator, and the dune buggy surged forward.

Dust spewed from behind the oversize rear tires, and Burke gripped his machine gun with both hands to keep from rocking too much in his seat. Another moment brought them to the clapboard shed, the driver swerving wide around it, keeping up his speed, while Burke was poised and ready for a target to reveal itself.

The Mexican surprised him even so. Instead of running for his life, he leaped out of the shadows, a revolver thrust in front of him at full arm's length, and squeezed off three quick rounds from less than twenty feet away. It was a miracle that he didn't score a killing hit at such close range, but he came close enough. One bullet grazed Burke's ribs, a second ricocheted from his machine gun's barrel and the third passed close enough beside his face that he could feel it stir his close-cropped hair.

Burke lost it then, the curses spilling out of him like some weird incantation as he swung around the .30-caliber MG to meet his would-be killer. Holding down the trigger, he unleashed a storm of bullets, hosing down the Mexican and lifting him completely off his feet, a man-sized piece of chaff caught by the wind. At that, the dead man got off one last shot before he hit the ground, the driver yelping as the bullet scorched a path across his thigh.

The buggy veered off course, came dangerously close to stalling, but the driver saved it at the final instant, spewing curses Burke had no room to condemn. He kept on going, cleared the back side of the shed, and Burke spied the other Mexicans he had been looking for. They were some twenty yards in front of him and running for their lives, two women and a child.

No matter. Nits made lice, the prophet always said. In the Old Testament, Yahweh ordered his chosen people to annihilate their enemies, down to the very youngest, so that none survived to flaunt his holy statutes. As it was in Saul's and David's time, so would it always be.

He shot the runners from behind, a sweep from left to right that dropped the three of them facedown like broken mannequins. At that, he almost missed the little boy, nearly forgot to make allowance for his height, but caught himself in time to nail the youngster with two bullets in the back.

The buggy's engine sputtered, coughed, regained its beat, then started gasping. Burke leaned forward, one hand braced on the machine gun, while his other found the driver's shoulder in a painful grip.

"What's going on?" he asked.

"I don't... Oh, shit! We're almost out of gas. They must've hit the goddamn tank!"

Burke had a sudden urge to punch the man for his profanity or for the bad news he delivered, but it wouldn't help in either case. He thought back to the first shot that had struck the buggy, shortly after they had burst into Colonia Verdad, and knew it had to have done the damage, draining precious fuel despite his swift retaliation on the man who fired the bullet. Any second now, they would be stranded and—

The engine died.

Burke couldn't take the Browning with him. It was useless to him now unless he lingered with the vehicle, and that would be a foolish choice, make him a sitting duck for any of his adversaries with a weapon and the will to use it.

It was time to cut and run.

"Come on!" Burke ordered, reaching down to grab his Ingram MAC-10 submachine gun as the buggy coasted to a halt. "We're getting out of here!"

PACO FIGUERAS COULDN'T find Emilio or their mother, and it frightened him. He didn't frighten easily, but the thought of losing his last relatives on earth made him feel dizzy, nauseous, as if he were about to faint.

He took another, deeper breath and held it for a moment, until the ringing in his ears subsided and his hands stopped trembling. He clutched the shotgun tighter, trying to draw strength from wood and steel.

As far as he could tell, the two shots he had fired so far had both been wasted. First, a dune buggy had nearly run him down as he was sprinting for the shelter of a hut on the perimeter, and Paco's parting blast had kicked up dust a yard behind the speeding vehicle. At that, the gunner in the vehicle had nearly cut him down, but Paco had evaded him, ducking and rolling, sliding into cover while Zinn's triggerman sped off in search of other targets.

In the excitement of his near-miss, Paco carelessly forgot to pump the shotgun's slide to chamber a new round. Some moments later, when he saw a pair of Nehemiah's foot soldiers approaching and stepped out to meet them, shouldering his weapon, taking up the trigger slack produced a sharp metallic click, but nothing else.

Paco nearly soiled himself in panic as the two cut loose with automatic weapons, firing from the hip. One of their bullets grazed him as he dived back for cover, cursing his own negligence. Still grimacing with pain, he pumped the shotgun but didn't dare stick his head around the corner for a well-aimed shot. Instead, he poked the shotgun's muzzle clear and triggered off a blast, then ran away without a backward glance to see if he had wounded either one of his assailants.

The remainder of his time had been spent searching for Emilio and their mother, but without result. Despair picked at his mind like the sharp, cruel beak of a carrion bird. What would he do without his family, assuming that he managed to survive the night? Was living even worth the trouble?

The silent answer to that question was an immediate, emphatic yes. Life was precious, even if he had to spend it by himself in bleak despair. Whatever happened, Paco was determined to survive.

Of course, it might already be too late. From all the evidence around him—dead and wounded bodies everywhere he looked, most of them friends and coreligionists of his—it was entirely possible that Zinn's commandos had the battle won, all finished but the mopping up. And yet someone was fighting back; that much was obvious to Paco from the sounds of gunfire ringing through the camp. It couldn't all be Zinn's assassins finishing the wounded. Scattered shots, perhaps, but not the echoes of explosions, the sustained bursts of machine-gun fire. He chose a compass point at random and began to move in that direction, watching out for enemies along the way.

He found his brother by dumb luck—or by the grace of God. Emilio was crouched beside the hut that housed their generator, half-surrounded by three gunmen wearing blue arm bands, Zinn's killers. They were closing in, relentless in their progress, though Emilio was doing all he could to hold them off, taking a pot shot now and then to keep their heads down, obviously trying to conserve his ammunition for the last, inevitable rush.

Paco saw red. The bastards were bent on murdering his only brother, while for all he knew their mother was already dead. It was intolerable. He would give his own life, if he had to, to protect Emilio.

No sooner had the notion sprung into his mind than it translated into action. Paco charged the nearest of Zinn's killers, bellowing a challenge on the run, his 12-gauge shotgun leveled from the waist. His rush surprised the gunman, brought his head around, the automatic rifle following a beat more slowly. Too slow, as it happened, for the man to save himself.

Paco fired a shotgun blast from less than twenty feet away, and there was no way he could miss at that range. Buckshot slammed into his target's chest and took the startled soldier down without a whimper, dead before he hit the ground. This time, Paco remembered what he had to do and pumped the shotgun's slide to put a live round in the chamber, veering toward the second of the three commandos, keeping up his breakneck pace.

This time, his target was forewarned, a weapon that appeared to be a Russian AK-47 pointed in the general direction of his head. Paco launched himself into a dive, triggering another blast while he was airborne, praying for a hit.

He got his wish. Zinn's soldier was staggered by the shock of spreading buckshot and dropped to one knee. Paco hit the deck with force enough to drive the air out of his lungs. He felt as if he were drowning, a sensation he recalled from youthful soccer games, when he would fall the wrong way, and he knew it wouldn't kill him—but his adversary would, unless he finished it without delay.

Lungs screaming, dark spots swimming in his field of vision, Paco pumped the shotgun once again, lined up his shot with more instinct than skill and squeezed the trigger. Even as the wooden stock slammed hard against his shoulder, Paco knew the shot was good. He didn't have to see his enemy vault over backward, spouting crimson from the ragged holes in his chest and throat.

That still left one, and he was lurching to his feet, trying to breathe and concentrating on his weapon, grappling with the slide, when bullets started kicking up the dust around him. Paco's final target had apparently forgotten all about Emilio, advancing toward the younger brother with long strides and firing from the hip. A bullet plucked at Paco's sleeve. Another stung his earlobe. He brought the 12-gauge to his shoulder, framed his target in the open sights and squeezed the trigger.

Click!

Damn it!

Desperately he worked the slide and tried again, with an identical result. The gun was empty. Paco hadn't counted as he fired each shot, and there was no time to reload.

A rifle bullet tore into his side, below his ribs, and twisted him off balance. Instantly another struck his left thigh, snatched the leg from under him and dumped him on his wounded side. A bolt of agony shot up his spine, exploding in his skull, and Paco knew that he was finished. He was dead.

But why, then, could he still hear shooting? And how was it that the AK-47's harsh, metallic banging shifted to a higher, sharper pitch?

His eyes swam into focus just in time to see Zinn's gunman topple forward, sprawling facedown in the dirt. Behind him stood Emilio, the M-1 carbine leveled at his waist. As Paco watched, he fired another round into the prostrate form and made the dead man twitch.

A moment later, and Emilio was kneeling at his brother's side. He cradled Paco in his arms, recoiling as his touch produced a breathless cry of pain.

"I'm all right," Paco gasped. "Help me up. We can't stay here."

Emilio felt hot tears of pride and fury coursing down his cheeks. With strength he didn't know that he possessed, he hoisted Paco to his feet and started looking for a place where they could make their final stand. The generator shed was too small, its plywood walls like cardboard to machine-gun bullets.

To his left, some fifty feet away, another Quonset hut stood waiting, its door ajar. Its corrugated metal wasn't bulletproof by any means, but it would have to do.

Grimly, with bitter resignation in their hearts, the brothers hobbled toward their final sanctuary, limping toward a rendezvous with death.

BOLAN HAD TAKEN OUT the fourth dune buggy with another frag grenade and finished off the wounded driver with a burst from the Uzi. The gunner's luck had failed him when he vaulted from the rolling vehicle, his neck snapping like a stick of balsa wood when he had landed on his head.

One desert rat-mobile remained, and he tracked it by the revving engine sounds, the rattle of machine-gun fire. Twice Bolan passed dazed members of the commune, none of them with guns. They shied away from him, and while one older woman crossed herself, none of them tried to run. It was as if they had accepted death and lacked the nerve or energy to make the Reaper work for his reward.

He concentrated on the buggy, watching out for snipers, meeting none. Ironically it struck him that the tide had turned just as the people of Colonia Verdad began to give up hope. He didn't care if the religious cult survived or not, but he had come this far in hopes of working out some kind of bargain with its leaders, and he wasn't ready to turn back.

Not yet.

He saw the buggy's headlights flashing in the darkness, glinting from the metal siding of a Quonset hut. Flame sputtered from the muzzle of the vehicle's machine gun, bullets clanging as they drilled through corrugated walls. The gunners in the dune buggy apparently had someone trapped inside the hut. Some kind of lightweight weapon answered the machine-gun fire, two quick rounds through an open window, wasted, there and gone before the shooter dropped back out of sight.

At least the sniper in the hut was a distraction, giving Bolan the diversion he required to close the gap between himself and the dune buggy. He was thirty yards away when the machine gunner reached down and came up with a round, dark object in his hand, roughly the same size as a baseball. He reared back to lob it through the same dark window that his adversary had been firing from a moment earlier.

Grenade!

The blast was muffled slightly, most of its destructive force contained inside the hut, although a tongue of flame licked through the open window briefly, and was gone. Smoke followed, pouring from the window and a nearby door that stood half-open. If the hut's defender was alive, he made no sound, denied his would-be killers any satisfaction they might otherwise have drawn from cries of pain.

Bolan was almost near enough to strike when gunfire stuttered from his left, a line of tiny dust devils erupting at his feet. He swung to face the enemy and saw another of the soldiers with a blue arm band advancing on him, scowling with a soot-stained face and spraying automatic fire from his Kalashnikov.

The Uzi whispered a reply, three rounds exploding from its bulky muzzle, tattooing their imprints on the target's chest. The gunner's scowl changed instantly, became a dazed and vaguely pained expression as he toppled over backward, triggering a last burst toward the desert sky.

Bolan didn't wait to observe his late opponent's fall. Almost before the dead man's knees had buckled, he was turning back to face the dune buggy, prepared to see the Browning .30-caliber MG aimed at his face, its triggerman alerted by the bursts of AK-47 fire.

But he hadn't been seen. Not yet. Instead, the gunner in the dune buggy was focused on a scarecrow figure just emerging from the smoky doorway of the hut. The figure held an M-1 carbine at port arms, not aiming it, a look that might have been shell shock or blinding fury on his face.

Whatever he was working on inside his head, it took too long. The gunner in the dune buggy was lining up his shot, already taking up the trigger slack, when Bolan stitched his right flank with a burst of parabellum shockers. Reeling, spilling precious blood from half a dozen wounds, the shooter tried to bring his piece around and take somebody, anybody, with him as his life ran out. He held down the Browning's trigger, the muzzle winking flame as armor-piercing slugs and tracers filled the air.

Bolan shot him again, the second burst chewing up his target's chest, throat, face, before it ripped him from his seat and dumped him from the vehicle and sprawled him on the ground.

The driver came alive to what was happening behind him, twisting in his seat and groping for the buggy's gearshift simultaneously. Whether he was trying to reverse the vehicle or simply find a lower gear to give himself some traction, Bolan never knew. He spent the last rounds from his Uzi's magazine to take the wheelman's face off, and the dune buggy lurched forward, struck the hut's bullet-riddled wall and stalled.

He turned to face the Mexican, who had his carbine pointed now at Bolan's chest. The rifleman said something, speaking Spanish, but when Bolan shook his head, he tried again.

"I don't know you."

"You will." The useless Uzi was a deadweight in his hands. He gauged the distance to his side arm, thinking maybe he could make it if the Mexican was slow enough.

"They've killed my brother." As he spoke, the dark man nodded toward the empty doorway at his back. "Perhaps my mother, too."

"We could go find her," Bolan said.

"Who are you?"

"Later," Bolan told him. "First things first."

The Mexican considered that for several heartbeats, finally nodded, lowering his weapon as he went to join the Executioner. Together, they moved off to search the battlefield.

Payback could wait awhile.

9

Emilio's mother wasn't dead. In fact, she had survived the raid without a scratch, although the carnage she had witnessed would leave scars no eye could see. They found her on the north edge of the camp, a dead child cradled in her arms, three panicky but otherwise uninjured youngsters clinging to her for protection in the smoky darkness.

Bolan had never taken time to count the enemies he killed. In Vietnam, where he had earned his nickname "the Executioner," he had been credited officially with ninety-seven kills, a total that excluded NVA and VC soldiers killed in jungle skirmishes on both sides of the DMZ. A few years later, in the midst of Bolan's one-man war against the Mafia, a Wanted poster issued by the FBI had named him as a suspect in one thousand unsolved homicides. He didn't know if that was accurate or an exaggeration by some federal bookkeeper, but there had been more killings since—a great deal more. He had spilled a lake of blood, and he wasn't finished yet.

But he had never grown immune to suffering among the innocents.

He had known cops and soldiers, many of them who were hardened to the sight, sound and smell of death, no matter who the victims were. They burned out from the killing, or from simply wading through the blood to do their jobs day after day, and something in their spirits—the essential spark of human kindness—joined the dead they left behind. For Bolan, it had never come that easy. While he rarely wept, at least where anyone could see him, he was still the same man who had worn another nickname in the living hell of Southeast Asia. Some who knew him then had dubbed him "Sergeant Mercy," for the times he carried wounded friends and enemies alike to field hospitals, risking life and limb along the way to see them safely home.

There was a doctor at Colonia Verdad, or so he claimed to be, and Bolan didn't question his credentials as he moved among the stricken, bandaging their wounds, probing for bullets here, setting a broken femur there, dispensing the few painkillers he had been able to retrieve from the infirmary before it burned. Bolan helped carry some of those who could not walk into the Quonset hut where the camp's medic operated by the light of kerosene lanterns, half a dozen women huddled in a corner, alternately chanting prayers or weeping for the dead and maimed.

"It could be worse," Emilio Figueras told him after they had worked together for the best part of two hours, picking up the pieces, checking bullet-riddled, burned-out huts for other victims of the raid.

That much was true. From what Bolan saw, some two-thirds of the compound's residents had managed to survive the blitz, and no more than a dozen to fifteen of those had suffered major wounds. The down side—Bolan guessed that nearly all the gravely injured ones would die from shock or loss of blood before they could be moved out to a proper hospital.

The compound had one flatbed truck and half a dozen ancient cars, but all of them had taken hits in the attack, and only two or three were drivable. If each of them was packed with wounded, it would still take two or three trips back and forth to Rosarito, where the nearest doctor plied his trade, and Bolan estimated that as many as one-third would die along the way.

It would be faster with a Medevac, of course, but there was still no sign of the authorities, and the camp's short-wave radio had been knocked out by machine-gun fire, along with the generator. Driving into Rosarito to report the raid would add another hour, minimum, to any kind of medical response time, meaning that the live-in doctor was, for all intents and purposes, the only game in town.

While he was working, Bolan and Figueras found a quiet corner of the compound for themselves and settled down to have a talk. Sporadic interruptions by survivors of the raid didn't prevent them from communicating man-to-man, one battle-scarred combatant to another.

"I owe you my life and many thanks," Figueras said when they were seated with their backs against the wall of a surprisingly undamaged Quonset hut, with pale dawn breaking in the east. "But I don't even know your name."

"Call me Belasko," Bolan told him. "Mike. It's good enough for now."

"I understand. How can I help you, now that you have done this unexpected service for my people?"

Bolan had decided in advance approximately how much he would share if he was able to communicate with those who ran Colonia Verdad. "I come from the United States," he said. "You worked that out already, I imagine."

"Yes."

"I'm working on a group that calls itself the Paul Revere Militia," Bolan said. "They're involved with acts of terrorism in the States. Until the night before last, they were also operating from a camp about an hour north of here, not far from Nehemiah Zinn's Colonia Cristo."

"I know the place," Figueras said with evident distaste. "You speak as if it is no more."

"They had some trouble," Bolan said, and let it go at

that. "The leftovers are hanging out with Zinn until they find another base camp."

"That explains it," Figueras said, nodding solemnly.

"Explains what?"

"The raid tonight. Zinn and his followers undoubtedly suspect my people for the raid you have described. Tonight was—what do gringos say?—the payback?"

"That's what gringos say." Figueras's statement took him by surprise, hit Bolan like a swift blow to the gut, but on reflection it seemed obvious. He had been thinking of bad blood between the two religious communes, earlier described to him by Ginger Ross, but it hadn't occurred to him that Zinn and Stone would draw their own conclusions from the first move of his Baja blitz. The pair of them had added two plus two, come up with five and launched a strike against the only local enemy they could identify.

Which meant that all the blood spilled at Colonia Verdad that night—to some extent, at least—was smeared on Bolan's hands.

That mental image sickened him, and Bolan swiftly put it out of mind. He changed the subject, shifting to the topic that had been his first concern as he approached the camp that night, before all hell broke loose.

"I'm told that Zinn and the militia trade in weapons, sometimes with the Zapatistas."

"You were told the truth. When I was at the colony, they shipped arms north *and* south, to anyone with the money in his hand. I thought it strange, that Zinn would trade with Communists and drug dealers when he claimed to be a Christian prophet. It was one of many things that finally prompted me to leave."

"I have no right to ask," Bolan said, "but it would be helpful if I could identify Zinn's contacts with the Zapatistas, maybe find out where he keeps his merchandise, that kind of thing."

"Then you're in luck," Figueras said, and smiled for the first time since meeting Bolan several hours earlier. It was a bitter smile, almost a grimace, prompted by his anger and a yearning for revenge. It gave his lean face the appearance of a grinning skull.

"How's that?"

"I have the names you need, and something more."

ZINN HAD EXPECTED casualties from the assault upon Colonia Verdad. In war, both sides expected losses on the battlefield. You couldn't make an omelette without breaking eggs, et cetera.

But it seemed impossible that no one would return from the attack. He couldn't deny that his commandos—every blessed one of them—were several hours late. They had been scheduled to attack Colonia Verdad at midnight, raise whatever hell they could in thirty minutes, give or take, then return to Zinn's command post and report. Drive time included, they should easily have reached Colonia Cristo by 2:30 or 3:00 a.m.

So where in hell were they?

The more he thought about it, Zinn considered that "in hell" was probably a nice, safe bet. Or, rather, he should say "in heaven," since the raiders had been sent to war for Yahweh's sake, to do God's dirty work as calculated by his prophet, Nehemiah Zinn. It all came out the same, in earthly terms.

His twenty men were dead.

Emilio Figueras was a more effective battlefield commander than he had anticipated. Far from rolling over, cringing while Zinn's soldiers kicked his ass, the Mexican had rallied somehow and wiped out the raiding party.

It would be doubly difficult to kill the little bastard now. He would be on his guard, for one thing, waiting for another try, seeing to his defenses. On the home front, Zinn would have a harder time convincing members of his flock to take part in another raid against Colonia Verdad. They wouldn't come right out in public and defy him—none of them were strong enough for that—but he could already imagine the pathetic grumbling they would do among themselves, behind his back, perpetuating a defeatist attitude. If they were frightened, if they lacked self-confidence and trust in Yahweh, trust in him, it gave Figueras and his scum a powerful advantage on the battlefield before another shot was ever fired.

Daybreak brought the grim survivors of Zinn's cadre slouching from their quarters, looking sour, disenchanted. Some of them had waited up until 4:30 a.m. to greet the raiders, hear their boasts of victory, and those were hollow-eyed from lack of sleep. On every side, Zinn picked out faces wearing looks that seemed to challenge his authority. How could the Prophet fail, they wondered, if he was in fact God's chosen one? Was it a sign? Yahweh's own retribution for some failing on Zinn's part? Could he be trusted to explain the loss, much less to make it right?

Zinn felt his paranoia peaking, cold sweat beading on his forehead, tickling like the tiny feet of insects on the flesh between his shoulder blades. His ears were ringing, and his fingertips were numb. If he began to speak right now, this moment, Zinn knew he would stammer as he had in childhood, when the other kids had called him "Porky Pig" in school.

He took a deep breath, held it and released it slowly. In his mind, he pictured Yahweh sitting on a massive golden throne beyond the clouds, observing everything that happened on the mud ball known as Planet Earth. Somehow, in his exalted wisdom, he had chosen Nehemiah Zinn from all the billions of potential candidates to lead a new revival and prepare the way for Christ's return in glory. He was smiling at his prophet now, and reaching out a hand the size of Texas, offering to shoulder any burden that his chosen minister on earth couldn't lift on his own.

"Brothers and sisters!" Zinn called out to his disciples, smiling as the words emerged without a trace of hesitation. "Rally here to me!"

They came when they were called, like any well-trained animals. Zinn stood before them on the dais they had built for him outside his quarters, shaded by a roof that would be more useful at midday than in the first hour after dawn.

"I have sad news," he said before they could begin to mutter, circulating rumors in the ranks. "Although we can't be positive just yet, it seems the Christian soldiers who were sent to do Lord Yahweh's work last night will not return to us. Unless I miss my guess, they're up in heaven with the master, even as we speak."

A couple of the women in the crowd were weeping, and there would be others in a moment, once the news sank in. Zinn didn't wait for them.

"Grieve not!" he shouted at his audience. "Fear not! 'Let not your hearts faint, fear not, and do not tremble, neither be ye terrified because of them. For the Lord your God is he that goeth with you, to fight for you against your enemies, to save you.' Deuteronomy 20, verses three and four."

A weak "Amen" came back at him from somewhere in the pack, barely a whisper, and he tried again. "Hebrews 9:27 tells us, 'It is appointed unto men once to die, but after this the judgment.' Is there any man among you here today who doubts the valiant service of these soldiers to our Lord?"

No hands were raised. Zinn thought he had them, now.

"If you were really faithful Christians, you'd rejoice that these men have gone on to their reward with Yahweh," Zinn continued, turning it around. "You'd join with Paul from 1 Corinthians, the fifteenth chapter, when he said, 'O death, where is thy sting? O grave, where is thy victory?'"

Perhaps a dozen voices cried "Amen" that time, with slightly more enthusiasm. Pastor Zinn was on a roll, his own depression vanishing in the rising swell of oratory.

"We're not finished yet!" he promised his assembled flock. "Not by a long shot! Those who gave their lives for us last night did not go down in vain! I swear to you that they will be avenged, no matter what it takes! At any cost! Our enemies will rue the godforsaken day they took up arms against the Lord of Hosts!"

Cheers from the audience, some fists raised in defiance of Figueras and his heretics.

"I mean to see our enemies ground underfoot and crushed like the unclean, pernicious vipers that they are!" Zinn thundered. "There's no place they can hide! 'And the smoke of their torment ascendeth up for ever and ever: and they have no rest day nor night, who worship the beast and his image, and whosoever receiveth the mark of his name.' Revelation 14:11."

"Amen! Amen!"

That was more like it. Zinn was smiling broadly as he stepped down from the dais, moved among them, patting shoulders, shaking hands, supplying words of comfort here and stiffening a backbone there.

He wasn't finished yet.

In fact, the truth was he had only just begun to fight.

STONE WISHED he could postpone the handoff, but it would have caused more problems down the road, perhaps disrupting commerce with the Zapatistas altogether. They were touchy, that crowd. If you failed them once, they held a grudge forever and were prone to act on it, not only take their business elsewhere but retaliate with violence if they saw an opportunity.

That was the problem with romantic revolutionaries, Stone decided. They were always hot to trot and burned out early, most of them already dead or locked up in a stinking prison before they reached the big three-o.

So he would keep his date with Altamiro, turn the weapons over and collect his cash. It was a damn good thing that he had stashed the guns with Zinn's religious loonies on a whim, instead of storing them at the militia compound, where they would have likely been destroyed along with nearly half his men.

Now Zinn had gone and taken his best shot at payback for the raid, assuming that the individuals responsible were Mexicans from the pathetic colony of losers who had walked out on his church long years ago, disgusted with the way he favored white disciples over local natives. All except the women, that is. Zinn had liked the Latin poon just fine, had even found a biblical text or two to ratify his bedding anything in skirts. Some crap about repopulating after an apocalypse, as if that should apply somehow to daily life in Baja.

Jesus H., but he was tired of dealing with fanatics, lunatics, and losers. Stone would almost have preferred to take a cut in pay and fight an honest war again, with men around him he could trust to do their jobs and keep their mouths shut, without spouting mindless nonsense every time they drew a breath.

Almost.

He was burned out on zealots and their causes, sick to death of rubbing shoulders with the dregs of a completely decadent society, but he was still addicted to the money. Stone was saving up for his retirement, looking at this mission as his last time in the field, his final journey under fire. The truth was, he had earned a rest. Some tropical climate, maybe lounging on a beach he didn't have to storm through flying bullets, with a cold drink in his hand and a warm body at his side. Perhaps two bodies, if it struck his fancy. And why not?

Stone had been all-out for his country in his younger days, before he understood that everybody from the White House down to the commissioned officers who told him where to go and whom to kill were busy looking out for number one. He had been stupid way back then, but that had changed. It took four tours of duty, but he finally wised up and struck off on his own, a gun for hire, and he had done all right. The modern world was always short of killers, people who could do the dirty work and walk away from it without a nervous breakdown. Stone was good at what he did—one of the best, in fact—and it was paying off.

But not without some risks.

Like now, for instance, running from an enemy whom he had yet to glimpse, much less identify or neutralize. There had been moments since the raid in Idaho when he had thought of simply disappearing, leaving Rahman to complete the work himself, if he was able, but it went against Stone's grain to cut and run.

And then again, there was the problem of attempting to elude a group like Hezbollah. They weren't omniscient, but they damn sure got around, and with the oil money of several Arab states behind them they could reach out to the farthest corners of the globe, locate a man who had convinced himself that he was safe and take him out while he was sitting down to breakfast. You never knew when they were coming for you, who would be the triggerman or woman, when you would go out to start your car and have the world explode around you.

Stone wasn't a coward. He had proved that countless times on several continents. The Arabs wouldn't have employed him in the first place if he let his fears control him, but he took pride in his grasp of common sense. It would be stupid to invite the lethal wrath of Hezbollah before he even knew whom he was dealing with and whether there was some way to eliminate the threat himself. Far better, if it came to that, for him to learn his adversary's name and pass it on to Rahman, let the Palestinians step in and lend a hand to get their precious operation back on track.

It had been damaged, granted, but it wasn't hopeless yet. The lady Fed could hurt them—hurt him, anyway—but agents from the FBI or ATF would have to get their hands on Stone before they could prevent him from proceeding with his plans. Those plans had been delayed, rerouted, but they weren't canceled, not by any means. He still had contacts in the States, much of the hardware was in place and he could push the buttons from a distance if he had to.

Part of Rahman's plan, from the beginning, had been setting up the Paul Revere Militia to receive the heat that emanated from their actions. Let the U.S. government and some of its most vocal enemies wage open warfare in headlines, yet another black eye for the nation that appeared to be disintegrating along ethnic, economic and political fault lines.

Ten years ago, Stone would have been among the first to grab a gun and drop Rahman on sight, go hunting for his minions in their dingy hiding places, but the days of taking orders and saluting flags had passed him by. He had become a mercenary in the strictest sense, prepared to kill for money, anytime and anywhere, without regard to who was picking up the tab. And by extension, Stone was theoretically prepared to die in the pursuit of cash, as well.

But not this day.

His goal in signing on with Rahman and the Hezbollah was to retire, not to expire. If he was simply looking for a one-way ticket to the cemetery, he could easily have found more pleasant ways to make the trip. Right now, he had the best part of a million tax-free dollars sitting in a numbered bank account, and there would be another two million when he had seen the operation through. With that kind of money, Stone imagined he could live quite nicely on the interest, have his cake and eat it, too, until he felt like really splurging in his golden years.

Assuming, always, that he lived that long.

If he was going to collect that last two million—or enjoy the money he already had, for that matter—Stone had to be alive. And to ensure that, he would have to take out his adversaries as soon as possible.

Which meant that he would have to find out who they were—or who *he* was.

Sometimes what you didn't know could hurt you.

Sometimes it could even get you killed.

10

Rosarito was the kind of town where white women stood out, particularly one who was without a man. It wasn't much on tourism—too far inland to draw the scuba divers, fishermen and such; no classic architecture for the culturally inclined; wild pigs and not much else to lure big-game hunters—and gringos who remained in town more than a day or two excited comment from the natives.

Ginger Ross had just about decided that the time had come for her to split. She had been wandering the sunbaked streets for two days running, trying to pretend that she was on the prowl for bargains, native art, whatever, and she hadn't glimpsed a single member of the Paul Revere Militia in that time. She hadn't glimpsed another Anglo, if the truth were known, since Mike Belasko left her at his rented digs the night before last and evaporated.

Ross wasn't terribly concerned about his safety—it was pretty obvious that he could take care of himself all right—but she would still have liked to know what he was doing, whether he was making any progress on the case she still thought of as hers.

No, that was wrong. She wasn't on a case these days. For all she knew, she might not even have a job. Her supervisor back at ATF headquarters had been steaming when she broke off contact and defied his orders back in Idaho... how long ago? Almost two weeks? Since then, the woman had been through hell and back, and she had nothing much to show for it except a motley bunch of cuts and bruises, plus a badly wounded ego.

Never mind.

She owed her partner something, owed his killers something else entirely, and she meant to pay those debts before she handed in her formal resignation. Not that any link to ATF, however tenuous, would help her in her present situation. She was well and truly on her own, apparently deserted even by the man who had retrieved her from the Paul Reveres. Belasko plainly wanted her to stay put at his rented flat—or better yet, head back to the United States and take her medicine—but she wasn't prepared to play along just yet.

No, thank you very much.

It could mean her career; she understood that. Hell, the job with ATF was lost already, if they went according to the book and held her to the letter of assorted regulations. Screw it. When she joined the bureau, she hadn't been thinking of retirement at the end of twenty years, a pension and a little cottage in Fort Lauderdale. The plan had been to do some good, help take some bad guys off the street before they had a chance to victimize the innocent. In that, Ross believed that she had been fairly successful—to a point. Her move against the Paul Revere Militia, with Jeff Frasier, would have been her crowning case to date, but they had blown it somehow. Jeff was dead, his body unrecovered, and her own career was hanging by a thread.

Across the keen edge of a razor, right.

Shit happens.

Ross would have laughed out loud if it weren't so serious. How many lives had the militia claimed while she was looking for the crucial bit of evidence that was required to bring them down? How many robberies and bombings had they perpetrated in the name of God and country? She couldn't begin to guess, but it was too damn many on all counts.

Which meant that she had failed so far.

With or without her badge, she still felt that she had a job to do. As for how she was supposed to finish it, however, the woman didn't have a clue.

What she did have, courtesy of Mike Belasko, was a pistol: a Ruger P-94 chambered for the same .40-caliber round—formerly known as 10 mm—that was standard for the FBI and spreading swiftly through the other branches of federal law enforcement. It had more knockdown power than your average 9 mm side arm, with a 12-round magazine and two spares on the side, together with a box of ammunition. While Belasko hadn't left her with an arsenal, he hadn't left her helpless, either.

It would have to be enough for now.

She knew the Baja players from her own investigation of the Paul Revere Militia and affiliated groups. She also knew that it would be the next best thing to suicide for her to make a run at them directly in their minifortress outside Rosarito. Stone would love to see her, get another chance at grilling her before he dropped her in a shallow grave, but that wasn't a part of Ross's plan.

The next time there were questions to be asked, she meant to do the asking, and with her interrogation by the Paul Reveres in mind, she told herself that she could be as rough as necessary. Take it all the way, with pistol-to-the-head techniques, if that was what she needed to produce a breakthrough.

It was liberating, in a strange way, being out of work. Without the badge, she didn't have a rule book to confine her, either. She wasn't concerned about the rules of evidence or warrants, whether someone on the other side complained that she was stepping on his rights. She wasn't even in America. Down here, the U.S. Constitution was a rumor, with no practical significance. You want to frame a copy, maybe hang it on the wall, it made a nifty decoration, but it had no relevance to anything that mattered.

In Mexico, police observed a rule they called the law of flight. In simple terms, it meant that any suspect running from the cops was subject to being shot and killed, regardless of his guilt or innocence. It didn't matter if you were suspected of jaywalking or premeditated murder. Try to make a break for it, and you were dead.

That rule didn't apply to gringo cops, of course, much less to those who had already lost their jobs by going AWOL and ignoring orders, but she was prepared to stretch a point. Chris Stone and his militia cronies had been running, more or less, since they had killed her partner back in Idaho. Stone had a bullet coming for the way that he had treated her, if nothing else. As for the rest, well, she had close to ninety rounds, and she was looking forward to the party.

It was good enough for Belasko, Ross thought, and it was good enough for her. If it turned out to be a fatal error, what the hell?

But first she needed information, and she knew exactly how to get it: find herself a member of the Paul Reveres off on his own, and take him into custody. Once they were somewhere nice and private, she could use the lessons Stone had taught her: squeeze until the bastard broke and told her everything he knew.

She finished packing and went out looking for a taxicab.

IT TROUBLED Aldo Altamiro, dealing with a pack of gringos for the arms his movement needed to survive, but fighting a guerrilla war required accommodation to unusual circumstances. Chairman Mao referred to the ideal guerrilla as a fish, his people as the ocean where the freedom fighter swam and fed and found his sanctuary. Anyone who helped the cause was welcome, even if it became necessary to destroy him later on for his reactionary views. Make use of everyone and everything, waste nothing and the victory was that much closer.

At that, the politics of his gringo collaborators worried Altamiro more than their pale skin. When they had first approached him through a native intermediary, he had balked at meeting them. The trap had seemed too obvious, transparent; any child would recognize that members of a paranoid, far-right militia group from the United States had to hate the Zapatistas, even as they hated Jews, blacks, feminists and all the others on their shopping list of enemies. It had to be some kind of trick, perhaps suggested to the army or the federal agents in return for sanctuary on the wrong side of the Rio Grande.

But it hadn't turned out that way, in spite of his original suspicions. Altamiro had been cautious, watching every move he made along the way, but the Americans were offering such weapons that he couldn't automatically and categorically refuse. They had M-60 light machine guns, M-16 and Mini-14 rifles, even the occasional M-79 grenade launcher and M-18 Claymore antipersonnel mines. Paying for the hardware was no problem, since the Zapatistas had survived for years on contributions and the proceeds from dramatic daylight robberies. If they ran short of money for a special shipment, they could always raid a bank or two to fatten up their treasury.

The hard part had been trusting Stone and his militiamen enough to keep that first appointment for the meeting that would lay down ground rules for their dealings yet to come. Neither pretended to admire the other's politics or ideology; they understood that any deal they struck would be a simple marriage of convenience, guns and weapons changing hands. As for sincerity, Altamiro believed that he could trust the gringos just as far as he could see them—if a pair of his men from the movement had them covered with an automatic weapon all the while.

Standard procedure.

Since he had joined the Zapatista movement seven years earlier, he had learned two vital lessons. First, that anyone, no matter how well-known or trusted for a lifetime, could turn out to be a traitor in the end. And second, that the strangest and most unexpected persons could turn out to be his friends, if only for an hour or a day. Thus, when a wealthy banker from Saltillo suddenly kicked in a contribution, he wasn't amazed. And when his cousin helped arrange a military ambush that claimed seven lives, it had been Altamiro and no other who disposed of him, a bullet in the head, his worthless body buried in an unmarked jungle grave.

He put the old news out of mind and started to look forward to his meeting with the gringos. They had special items for him this time, if Stone hadn't been exaggerating. Three more crates of M-16s, five thousand rounds of ammunition, eight LAW rockets, blasting caps and 250 pounds of C-4 plastic explosive. With that kind of equipment, Altamiro's cadre would be a force to reckon with, able to teach the soldiers and the federal agents what it meant to live in fear.

There was a risk, of course, in striking at the very targets that protected Stone and his militia. Gringos called it biting the hand that feeds you, but Altamiro had no interest in their homilies. His war was with the government of Mexico, and Stone was well aware of that. The gringo couldn't logically expect him to take the weapons he had purchased and secrete them in some warehouse, leaving them to gather rust and mold. Stone knew the Zapatistas were acquiring weapons and explosives for a reason; he knew what that reason was. If he was worried by the risks involved, then he should find another way to earn money.

Simple.

For the following day's meeting, Altamiro meant to pull out all the stops. He had a stolen truck on standby, fitted out with altered license plates, a driver with a Teamster's license and a team of reinforcements adequate to guard the arms once they were safely in his hands. If Stone had any sly tricks up his sleeve—if he had been establishing a cover all this time, for instance, setting up Altamiro for what the gringos would have called a sting—he would be sorry.

No. He would be dead.

Eleven men with automatic weapons would be covering the handoff, some of them from hiding, so that the Americans would be covered if they tried one of their underhanded tricks. He hoped that everything would be all right, but if it wasn't, well, whatever happened, Altamiro and his soldiers wouldn't go to prison, and they wouldn't die alone.

"Be quiet, now," he told the men who stood and sat around him, watching as he spread a hand-drawn map before them. It depicted the location where they were supposed to meet the Americans, the location of each soldier marked in red.

The Zapatista leader waited until he was sure he had their full attention, then he said, "We're going through this one more time."

CAPTAIN RODRIGUEZ FELT his stomach churning at the smell of death, but he couldn't allow his face to register the sickly feeling. It was his job to project an image of control, present himself to victims and to criminals alike as someone who had seen it all and was impervious to shock. The truth of it—that he was deeply troubled by the scene laid out before him, almost to the point of fearing he might lose his lunch—could never be revealed to anyone, or he would lose respect, control, the very basis of his rank.

In truth, Rodriguez thought he *had* seen everything, or

nearly so, from rape and robbery to random murder and political assassination. In his time, he had investigated human sacrifices and the vigilante execution of suspected witches. He had walked the bloody ground where Indians were massacred by men who craved their land for grazing cattle, or who simply hated them because their skin was red. He was familiar with the drug trade and the violence that it spawned, though he and his superiors were often paid—and rather handsomely, at that—to look the other way.

But this was different.

For the second time in twenty-four hours, Rodriguez stood in the midst of carnage on a scale that he had seldom witnessed, even in the backwash of guerrilla warfare that had always plagued his country. Two grim massacres, with more than fifty people dead between the two, and simple logic told him that the crimes had to be related. First, some unknown enemy attacked the camp where members of the Paul Revere Militia lived and trained, compelling the survivors to move in with the Reverend Zinn at Colonia Cristo. Then, the next night, yet another attack—this time against the members of a sect that had abandoned Zinn to form their own religious commune, not without much bitterness between the two.

A blind man could have seen that the events were linked, but what did that prove? Some of those who had been killed the previous night, while trying to annihilate Colonia Verdad, would almost certainly turn out to be members of Zinn's community. That posed a further problem for Rodriguez, since he had been bribed to leave Colonia Cristo alone and let the gringo zealots carry on as they saw fit. Until that week, it had been no great problem. All Rodriguez had to do was turn his back whenever guns were being transferred to the Zapatistas or across the border into the United States. The rebels weren't his problem, technically—they were a matter for the military—and Rodriguez didn't give a damn how many gringos killed one another in America.

In truth, even the local bloodshed he had witnessed in the past two days was more an inconvenience than a tragedy. When so many people were wiped out at once, it made the papers, and publicity in turn attracted politicians, with their secretaries and committees, nosing into things that would be better left alone. It was the same whenever a narcotics agent from the States was killed in Mexico, all sound and fury for a time, with everyone pretending that they meant to solve the case, reform the system, but the limits of their zeal involved the sacrifice of some policeman, or perhaps an army officer, who had become expendable.

Rodriguez feared that this time it might be his turn. He had observed the standard guidelines of the bribe, following his orders, sharing any payoffs he received with those who could protect him if the whole thing started to unravel, but the very basis of the system was a kind of faith—in money, in the honor of dishonorable men, in the propriety of persons whom you obviously couldn't trust. It was a fragile system, but it had survived for centuries by giving up its weaklings on occasion, offering a sacrifice or two to guarantee the common good.

The bodies had been sorted at Colonia Verdad, attackers off to one side, stacked without regard to dignity, while martyred residents of the religious commune were lined up behind two Quonset huts, where they were somewhat shaded from the sun. Rodriguez stood before the line of bodies covered by blue plastic tarpaulins and counted the protruding feet. Men on his left, then women, with the children to his right.

Only the children troubled him to any great extent. He told himself they had no future anyway; they had been peasants, growing up in a religious cult whose teachings would have kept them from succeeding in the modern world in any case. The last thing that his country needed at the moment was another generation of pathetic sheep who pledged their lives to following some self-styled holy man into a life-style that was hardly different from indentured slavery.

Still, they were children, all but one of them barefoot, bare legs or faded denim jeans protruding from beneath the tarp. The captain felt a sudden urge to kill the man who had done this, but he was already too late. The triggermen were dead themselves, and they hadn't died easily.

Good riddance.

Dealing with the man or men who sent them out to do this thing would be another matter, though. A public scandal might result if he went back to Zinn with accusations or arrest warrants and tried to charge the man with conspiracy. Zinn was a madman who believed himself anointed by God. If he was taken into court, he might say anything, reveal his dealings with the federal police, politicians, even with the Zapatistas. If that happened, heads would roll, and first among them would be his, for putting Zinn in a position where he felt obliged to talk.

There might be other ways to punish this atrocity, but Rodriguez would have to think about it and consult with his superiors before he made a move. And even if, against all odds, he was allowed to deal with Zinn, that still wouldn't resolve the question of the first raid, on the Paul Revere encampment. Zinn wasn't responsible for that, by any stretch of the imagination. The militiamen were his good friends—some of them even shared his strange religious notions—and it made no sense that they would run to hide out at Colonia Cristo if Zinn had been the one who killed their comrades hours earlier.

Which meant that he still had a mystery to solve, and it

wouldn't be simple. Long before he had a solid clue to work with, it was likely that more corpses would accumulate, more blood and more reporters, making his life miserable. He was in the middle of a war, with one side unidentified as yet, which made it difficult—if not impossible—for him to head off further violence. He would have to wait and see what happened next, if it wasn't too late to keep the whole damn thing from spreading like a wildfire in dry grass.

Whatever he was forced to do, the captain was determined not to let himself get burned.

11

The handoff had been scheduled for a site five miles above the border that divided Baja, north and south. Bolan showed up two hours early, looking for a vantage point, and found one in the jagged rocks overhanging an unpaved road that barely qualified as two lanes wide. Unmarked on any map, it was the kind of track that smugglers loved and law-enforcement officers patrolled at risk to life and limb.

He had no reason to believe that any cops would be along this morning to disturb the arms transaction. Given the remote location, plus the fact that they had probably been paid to stay away, it would require a terribly determined—or foolhardy—officer to show up uninvited at the meet.

There was an outside chance, of course, that one or more policemen would be brought along to keep the peace. Unlikely as it seemed, Bolan was forced to think about the possibility. He had a private rule against employing deadly force where lawmen were concerned, regardless of their individual corruption or brutality, and he would have to do some hasty shuffling of his plans if any uniforms turned up. That possibility aside, however, Bolan thought he was prepared for anything.

Decked out in desert camouflage, with war paint covering his exposed skin, he nestled in the shadow of a granite boulder. His main weapon was an M-16 A-2 with an M-203 grenade launcher attached, while bandoliers of extra magazines and 40 mm antipersonnel grenades were slung across his chest. The massive Desert Eagle semiautomatic on his right hip nearly doubled as a second rifle, while the black Beretta 93-R in his shoulder rig was capable of either semiauto fire or 3-round automatic bursts. He had removed the 93-R's custom sound suppressor for this occasion, thereby bettering the pistol's range and accuracy, since he didn't plan on any stealthy kills.

This day would be all blood and thunder once he put the ball in play.

He waited, sweating in the desert heat and trying to ignore it, watching as a scorpion came out to walk around the rock six inches from his face. He waited until the creature turned its back, then flicked it with his index finger, dropping it three yards to the dirt road below.

He heard the vehicles at 10:45 a.m., a quarter hour early, approaching from the south. That had to be the Zapatistas coming for the pickup, maybe scouting out the scene, alert for any signs of an impending ambush. Rebels stayed alive by giving free rein to their paranoia, trusting no one. Even after various successful dealings in the past, they would expect some treachery from Stone and company at every contact...but there was no way they could have reckoned on a visit from the Executioner.

That was Bolan's edge, his handle.

Scooting back another foot into the shadows, he prepared to meet the enemy.

RICHARD MCCAULEY had been startled and excited when the captain chose him as the pointman for the arms delivery. Stone usually handled things like that himself when he was in the area, but he had other business to take care of. And with Tracy dead, that left McCauley, with his brand-new sergeant's stripes, as second-in-command. It was a heady feeling—and a little worrisome—but he was confident that he could handle it.

They had been dealing with the Zapatistas for about two years now, well before McCauley came to Baja, running from indictments in New Mexico. At first, it had disturbed him that the Paul Reveres were doing business with a bunch of rebels he had always thought were godless Commies, but in time he came to understand the way things worked. The truth, he realized, was that it didn't matter what went down in Mexico. The government was a pathetic, socialistic mess already, the economy so screwed up that the natives were evacuating by the thousands every day, pouring into the United States, while jobs that used to be American went south, delivered on a crystal plate to peasants who would work for twenty cents an hour. If the wetback government came under fire, and ZOG decided on another bailout from the U.S. Treasury, so much the better. Maybe folks back in the States would finally wake up and smell the coffee, come to understand that they were being screwed without a kiss by their elected leaders.

And the day was coming when the Paul Revere Militia would be standing by to make it right.

But first, McCauley had a job to do.

He saw the Zapatistas waiting for him when he came around the last bend in the narrow, unpaved road, his old Ford Bronco followed by a Chevy pickup with the hardware in the back, beneath a tarp, a Land Rover with four more soldiers bringing up the rear. That gave him nine guns altogether, plus his own, and from the looks of things, the Mexicans had brought about the same.

McCauley double-checked the Ingram he was carrying, made sure it had a live round in the chamber and fiddled with the safety until he was satisfied that gentle pressure from his thumb would leave the little SMG ready to rip. The other men were likewise armed with AKs, SMGs or shotguns, but he wondered, looking at the Zapatistas now, if it would be enough.

He ordered himself to calm down. After two years of dealing with the rebels, there hadn't been a problem yet. Aldo Altamiro's people took their guns and paid in cash, the way they were supposed to, right on time. If they were something less than sociable at the exchanges, well, what difference did it make? Who wanted to waste time carousing with the wetbacks, anyway?

"Slow down," McCauley told his driver, Bobby Clark, then realized the Bronco was already slowing. Clark had made these runs before and knew the drill. Still, as the man in charge, McCauley felt he should say something to the troops. To satisfy the urge, he raised the plastic walkie-talkie to his lips and told the other members of his team, "Heads up."

The Mexicans had parked in such a way that they completely blocked the road, their flatbed turned around so that the tailgate faced McCauley's little convoy. It was easier for loading that way, and the truck was pointed in the right direction if they had to make a run for it, in case something went wrong. A beat-up station wagon and some kind of foreign two-door compact painted primer gray made up the rest of Altamiro's rolling stock. The Zapatista leader stood beside the station wagon, while his men fanned out across the road with rifles in their hands, resembling some kind of peasant firing squad.

Stone had advised McCauley that he didn't have to count the money Altamiro gave him. All he had to do was take the duffel bag and help the Mexicans unload the hardware they had purchased, making sure that no more than one-quarter of his soldiers laid their weapons down at any given time. When they were finished with the transfer, they were to turn around and drive back to the commune, where Stone would be waiting for him, taking care of more important things with Zinn.

No sweat.

Unless something went wrong.

McCauley pushed that prospect out of mind and concentrated on the raw mechanics of his mission, running down the mental checklist. Keep it simple. Greet the wetbacks. Get the money. Help them load the guns. Go home. A fucking idiot could handle it.

The Bronco stopped, but Clark left the engine running, as agreed. There was no point in taking chances. Gritty dirt crunched underneath McCauley's combat boots as he stepped out, the Ingram dangling by a shoulder strap so that it bumped against his hip. If Altamiro and the others took offense, to hell with it. They had enough guns showing on their side to stage another raid against the Alamo.

The moment that McCauley dreaded most was coming up: the handshake. For a couple seconds there, while he was squeezing Altamiro's paw, the Ingram would be useless to him. It reminded him of some old gangster movie he had seen on television when he was a little kid. Three goons walked in a flower shop and greeted the owner, smiling at him as if he were their long-lost brother. One of them stuck out his hand, and when the florist went to shake it, suddenly the pointman had him in a death grip, while the other two pulled .45s and blew his ass off, standing there among the roses and petunias. Ever since then, Dick McCauley had been careful shaking hands.

The Zapatista leader was approaching him, not smiling, but at least he seemed relaxed. If they were setting up some kind of sting, McCauley would have looked for little worry lines around his mouth and eyes. Of course, you couldn't always tell with other races. They could hide things better than a white man sometimes. Fake you out and rob you blind while you were trying to decide if they were saying "How are you?" or "Stick it up your ass."

The handshake, brisk and dry, was a relief. McCauley cocked a thumb back toward the Chevy pickup, telling Altamiro, "We've got what you need." And he couldn't resist a little smile, like in the movies, as he added, "I believe you've got something for me."

"Indeed." The Mexican spoke English like a native, and better than some. No accent that McCauley could discern, but then again, one word was nothing much to go on.

Altamiro snapped his fingers without looking back, and one of his men reached inside the foreign compact, coming back out with an OD duffel bag. McCauley didn't know exactly how much cash was in the bag, but it looked fairly heavy, even though the Mexican supported it one-handed.

What the hell. If he could do it, then McCauley—

Bang!

It was impossible to tell exactly where the first shot came from, but it dropped the Zapatista with the duffel bag as if someone had whacked him with a ball peen hammer. Blood and brains went flying as he vaulted over backward in the middle of the roadway, and the money bag he carried landed in the dirt.

McCauley gaped at the dead man, was just about to glance back toward his people when he saw the Mexicans reacting. They had to think the shot had come from his side, judging from the direction it had taken and the target. *Had* it? If someone on his team was flipping out and jeopardizing all their lives—

The second shot came out of nowhere, and someone gave a yelp of pain behind McCauley. One of his guys got hit that time. McCauley had been staring at the Mexicans, hadn't seen any of them fire that shot, but Altamiro could have people hidden in the rocky crags that flanked the road. It would explain why he was early, setting up his stand.

But what about that first shot?

All at once, guns opened up on both sides of the line. McCauley clutched at his Ingram even as he dodged back toward the Bronco, seeing Altamiro turn and run. The money lay between them, out in no-man's-land, beyond his reach.

McCauley knew he was in trouble, already wondering what Captain Stone would say.

And wondering if he would be alive to hear it.

BOLAN SIGHTED ON the Chevy pickup, with corrosion eating through both fenders on the driver's side, and knew the military hardware slated for delivery to the Zapatista rebels had to be hidden underneath that camo tarp. Two men crouched on either side of it, firing short bursts toward the Zapatista crowd.

Instead of strafing the truck, he lined up with the M-203 launcher mounted underneath the barrel of his rifle, stroked the chunky weapon's trigger and dispatched a 40 mm high-explosive round from fifty feet away. Its point of impact was above the Chevy's fuel tank just behind the forward gunner on that side, and when it blew, the shock wave pitched him over in a boneless somersault. The HE round and pickup's gas tank went so close together that it was effectively impossible to gauge the time lapse in between explosions: a smoky thunderclap erupting into brilliant, fiery streamers as the fuel caught and went everywhere, enveloping the soldiers who were close enough to feel the heat.

In other circumstances, Bolan might have favored them with mercy rounds to ease their suffering, but he was too busy at the moment. Downrange, there were at least fourteen or fifteen gunmen still alive and well, and some of them at least had worked out that the hostile fire they suffered wasn't coming from the other side, but from the hillside. Those were looking for a different kind of cover, putting vehicles between themselves and Bolan's roost, instead of simply dodging bullets from the people they had driven there to meet.

Before the rest of them could all catch on, the Executioner thumbed another 40 mm round into the breech of his grenade launcher, locked up and chose a target on the Zapatista side. The drab gray compact took his hot round through the windshield, seemed to swell as the grenade went off inside, then turned itself into a giant antipersonnel device, with jagged, rusty shrapnel flying everywhere.

He couldn't have it all his way, however, and both sides were firing back at him by now, some of them still exchanging short bursts with one another on the side. He could imagine what his enemies were thinking, the militiamen and Zapatistas each suspecting that the other had a sniper on the hillside, losing faith in that hypothesis as he began to fire on both sides indiscriminately. Still, they were unable to go back, start trusting one another as they had before the shooting started.

Not that there had ever been real trust between them in the first place. That was Bolan's ace, his hole card, and the wedge that he had driven in between their forces with two well-placed rifle shots.

And now all hell was breaking loose.

The first shots fired in his direction were reflexive, no real aiming, and they rattled off the crag above him without posing any real threat to the Executioner. He ducked back slightly when the bullets started coming closer, several of his adversaries taking time to aim, but they were still disorganized and dueling with one another on the side.

There would be no time like the present for him to cash in on that confusion, make it work for him and turn the momentary chaos to his own advantage.

Bolan reached back to his web belt, freed a hand grenade, released the safety pin and let the bomb fly in the direction of the Zapatista vehicles. The compact was already shattered, laying down a heavy smoke screen to obscure his human targets, but he didn't have to aim with the grenade, just let it fall among them and proceed to do its work.

He ducked back under cover, counting off the seconds until another thunderclap reverberated from the killing ground. The blast was followed closely by a sound of wailing voices, someone wounded or pretending to be injured, calling for relief. A trap? It made no difference, since he didn't plan on going down to face his targets at the moment.

Not until it came to mopping up.

The Paul Revere Militia's Land Rover was trying to escape, the engine grinding, catching on reluctantly, the driver shifting it into reverse. It looked as if three men were in the vehicle, but there could easily have been more hunched below his line of sight. Regardless of the numbers, though, he didn't want them going anywhere.

The first short burst from Bolan's M-16 took out the right front tire and chewed a few holes in the fender, several of his 5.56 mm tumblers rattling around beneath the Rover's hood and playing havoc with the engine wires and hoses. Wisps of pale gray smoke began to bleed from underneath the hood now, as the driver shifted to reverse and tried his best at backing out of there with one flat tire.

It was a risky proposition, but he might have made it to the first curve and out of range if Bolan hadn't aimed his next burst at the windshield. Glass exploded as his bullets chewed a course across the windshield, left to right, and found the startled faces just behind the glass. He saw the Rover lurch and stall, a dead foot slipping off the clutch, the engine flooding out and sputtering to silence.

Instantly, before the dust had even settled from the Rover's short trip in reverse, one of the rear doors opened to disgorge a diving, rolling figure dressed in camouflage fatigues. The self-styled soldier held some kind of stubby automatic weapon crushed against his chest, high-stepping as he gained his feet and broke for cover on the same side of the road where Bolan had his vantage point.

If he got there, the warrior thought, there would be at least some chance that he could work his way uphill and try to flank the adversary who was dumping so much hell onto his comrades and the Mexican commandos.

If he got there.

Bolan made sure that he didn't, leading slightly with his M-16, allowing for the angle of descent before his index finger drew back the trigger. Four, five, six rounds flew from the muzzle of his weapon, two of them completely wasted, but the other four went home with solid smacking sounds, as of a tenderizing mallet striking meat.

The chunky runner lost his stride, appeared to hook one foot behind the other, throwing one arm out in front of him as he began to fall. It didn't help, with bullets in his stomach, lungs and liver, but it was some kind of reflex that prevented him from going down without at least some minimal attempt to catch himself.

It didn't work, and he went down headfirst, his face plowing into dirt and gravel. There was still enough fight left in him to bring him up on hands and knees, but it was all for show, a dying spasm, and he soon collapsed again, to move no more.

As if on cue, the hostile fire from down below redoubled, much of it more accurate than before, and Bolan slid back under cover, waiting for the storm to pass. They didn't have him yet by any means, and cornering the Executioner could be a lethal hazard in itself.

If the survivors played their cards right, they might soon

have him surrounded in his stony niche.

And then, God help them all.

THE TASTE OF SMOKE and desert dust was foul on Aldo Altamiro's tongue. He clutched his AR-18S, an automatic carbine version of the Armalite AR-18 assault rifle, complete with folding stock, a shortened barrel, flash hider and forward pistol grip. Despite its rough appearance as a cut-down submachine gun, it still chambered the same 5.56 mm rounds as any other Armalite or M-16, which made it lethal at a hundred yards or better in the proper hands.

And it was in those hands this day.

Altamiro hadn't squeezed off a single shot so far, since he didn't believe in wasting ammunition on a target he had never seen. There might be situations—in a drive-by, for example, or if he was cornered in a house by troops outside—when he would spray the field with lead and keep his fingers crossed, but this was different. They were up against at least one enemy who knew what he was doing, who had decent weapons and the nerve to use them without thinking twice, but he was still up there, among the rocks, while Altamiro and his men retained some measure of mobility.

Which made him think that it was time for him to flee.

One thing about guerrilla warfare that appealed to Altamiro: there were no hard rules that everyone was honorbound to follow, under penalty of public shame or worse. The basic law was hit-and-run, harass and fade away to strike again some other place, some other day—and that meant there was no disgrace in running from a battle that was doomed to end in failure, possibly annihilation of your side. Conventional military minds would attribute such retreats to cowardice, brand them as failure, possibly deserving of a prison sentence or a firing squad, while the guerrilla master viewed the tactic as inspired, a way of living to protract the war, exacting further vengeance on your enemies.

Unfortunately for his men, it would be too conspicuous if Altamiro took them all along with him, when he retreated from the field. He was the leader, and it was imperative that he preserve himself for other battles—to avenge this craven ambush first, and take it on from there to greater heights of carnage. It was only fitting that his men should fight a rearguard action, cover his retreat, but they could do that just as well without the burden of oppressive knowledge that their leader had been called away.

They were already firing toward the hillside as it was, a couple of them still unloading on the gringos, too, though Altamiro understood by now that Stone and company weren't responsible. Or if they were, the leaders of the Paul Revere Militia had been wise enough, ruthless enough, to sacrifice their point team, make it look as if the sniper on the hillside had it in for both groups equally.

That part of it would take some thinking over, maybe consultation with his key advisers back at headquarters, but there was nothing he could do about it at the moment. First, he had to make his way out of the shooting gallery and find his way back to the fortress compound where his officers and men were waiting for him to return.

With that in mind, he started edging slowly backward, taking care to keep the station wagon squarely in between him and the hillside gunman. Altamiro had convinced himself that there was only one man firing on them from the slope. If there had been a cross fire, two or more such snipers working, he and all his soldiers would be dead by now.

It was a shame to lose the money and the guns, but this was one of those peculiar situations where it was enough to simply get out with your life. Accept the simple luxury of breathing as your just reward and spend the first days of your new life tracking down the enemy who had embarrassed you, then choose a time and place in which to pay him back tenfold.

He made it to the tailgate of the station wagon, hesitated long enough to see another of his men picked off, a bullet ripping through his bearded face, propelling him against the station wagon's fender with sufficient force to rock the long car on its springs.

And there would never be a better time to make his move, thought Altamiro as he turned and ran for cover on the far side of the unpaved highway, fading into shadows where the overhang of granite sheltered him and tall, dry weeds obscured his passage. Sixty yards or so beyond the ambush site, the road turned left, or eastward, and he would be safe. The sniper couldn't see him there, much less reach out and drop him with a bullet that pursued men around corners.

Various sensations jostled for supremacy in Altamiro's mind—rage was the most apparent, followed closely by disgust, confusion, and a wriggling little worm he recognized as fear. But as he left the killing ground behind him, one emotion rapidly eclipsed all others, left him almost giddy as he jogged along the roadside, shoulders hunched to take advantage of the uncut weeds.

That one emotion was relief.

THE EXECUTIONER WAS TIRED of playing with his prey, concerned that even on this isolated desert track, some innocent spectator or a local constable might suddenly appear to change the whole equation. One side or the other would be sure to grab a hostage, use the new arrival for a human shield if possible—or then again, a cop might try to intervene and get himself killed in the process, riddled by both sides. And if the cops who showed up on the scene were Feds, bought and paid for by his enemies, what then?

The time had come to wrap it up as efficaciously as possible, without delay. To that end, Bolan primed his M-203 launcher with another high-explosive round and swung to face the Zapatista team, fixed his sights on the station wagon that had carried backup gunners to the rendezvous and let his missile fly.

It was another perfect hit, impacting just behind the driver's door and blowing inward, so the car was nearly cut in two. The fuel tank ruptured, but it took another moment for the spilling gasoline to catch a light, then members of the strike team started running for their lives, some beating at the hungry flames that had already fastened to their clothes.

That left the flatbed truck, already sitting in a pool of flame that licked around the muddy tires and lapped beneath the chassis, seeking fuel to whet its appetite. A short burst from his rifle cored through the flatbed's tank and sent a dark cascade of diesel fuel to meet the flames. This time, when the explosion came, one of the Zapatista gunmen stood his ground, unloading on the Executioner's position with an SMG until the fire rolled up behind him, folded him into itself and swallowed him alive.

Bolan swung back to face the handful of surviving Paul Reveres. This would have been the time to move among them, looking for a coward or a wounded soldier he could squeeze for information, but he didn't want to speak with them. This was a killing mission, plain and simple, to disrupt Stone's dealings with the Zapatistas and deprive both sides of something they had craved.

He worked efficiently, almost mechanically, to flush the soldiers out and drop them in their tracks. He had already calculated there could be no more than five militiamen alive down there, and it turned out that he was off by one. The four who still remained when Bolan turned his full attention back to them were beaten men, and he could easily have let them slip away to tell the tale, spread fear among their comrades back at Colonia Cristo, but it simply wasn't in the cards.

Not this time.

Not these soldiers.

Bolan slammed a 40 mm HE round into the Bronco, thus depriving them of cover, and he had them covered when they came out firing. To their credit, they didn't throw down their weapons, raise their hands, try pleading for their lives. They weren't much on coordination, but they did their best, and Bolan aimed for quick, clean kills, no point in falling back on butchery. When he was finished, and the battle smoke began to clear, no one was moving on the field.

It was a wipe, but Bolan wasn't finished yet. The Zapatistas had another lesson coming to them, courtesy of Chris Stone and the Paul Revere Militia, and they hadn't seen the last of Bolan yet.

Not by a long shot.

12

No one was more surprised than Aldo Altamiro when he made it back to camp alive. He had been forced to walk the first six miles, afraid each time a car or pickup truck passed that it would be one of his enemies pursuing him, but he had finally relaxed enough to flag a ride as far as San Ignacio and walked again from there until a member of his own team recognized him, driving by, and stopped to take him home.

There was dismay and fury in the compound as he told his story, fudging only on the nature of his own departure from the battleground. As Altamiro told the story, his loyal men had pleaded with him to get out of there and save himself before it was too late. Reluctantly, reminded that the movement needed him in order to survive, he had agreed to swallow pride and leave the field.

Or so he said.

The truth about his flight from danger would have shamed him in the eyes of those who had to fear and serve him, if the movement was to carry on with the momentum it had gained in recent years. Altamiro was vital to the effort—anyone among his soldiers would have said as much, without a second thought. And yet if they had seen him creeping from the field of combat like a frightened rookie, hiding in the weeds and shadows, running with his tail between his legs, some might have changed their minds.

As for himself, Altamiro saw no real difference between

self-interest and the interest of the Zapatista movement. It
wasn't a selfish thing for him to save himself; rather, it
would have been a self-indulgent sin to throw his life away
on some heroic gesture that would further guarantee his
place in legend, while the movement lost one of its greatest
leaders of all time.

He could talk himself into believing damn near anything
if he tried hard enough.

Right now, though, the priority was beefing up security
around the Zapatista camp, in case the individuals responsible for the humiliating ambush weren't finished yet. It
seemed ridiculous, but he couldn't escape the notion that
his enemies might have pursued him somehow, followed
him back to his stronghold. Were they staring at him from
the darkness even now? If so, what could he do about it?
How could he protect himself?

He started off by doubling the guards around the camp
and telling them to stay alert. This was no drill, and they
had only to remember martyred friends to realize how serious he was. Most of them were mere peasants, but they
were honorable men, and all of them had been through
paramilitary training with instructors bribed away from military service. Most of them had fought against the government, spilled blood or had their own blood spilled, and they
weren't afraid of combat.

Not afraid.

The phrase made Altamiro scowl and cringe a bit inside,
but he concealed his feelings, taking extra pains with his
inspection of the camp and barking orders at his soldiers
with renewed ferocity. They didn't argue, taking to their
posts with something like excitement, as if looking forward
to a fight.

They hadn't seen the ambush at the border, though. They
hadn't watched their comrades die. It was one thing to cry
for vengeance, quite another to be witness at the incident

itself and then have time to think about your options, whether *you* would voluntarily trade places with the dead.

Or whether it was best to simply run away.

Three hours after he returned to camp, Altamiro believed they were as ready to defend the place as they would ever be. He hoped that it would be enough, hoped even more devoutly that they wouldn't need to fight. With any luck, he thought, the ambushers might take his money and his guns, be satisfied with what they had and leave the Zapatistas alone.

BOLAN HAD GLEANED coordinates for Altamiro's hideout from a phone call placed to Stony Man before the border ambush, after he left Ginger Ross back at the Rosarito safehouse. When he finished mopping up Stone's soldiers and the Zapatista troops, he knew exactly where to go and how to get there, but he took his time. A daylight strike against a well-armed camp wasn't his first choice for a winning strategy. He dawdled, stopped for food and gas along the way, pulled off the road at one point for a short nap in the car. It felt like sleeping in an oven, even with the windows down and back doors open, but he had survived worse in his day and would again.

With any luck at all.

The Zapatista camp was south of San Ignacio, in hilly country where the vegetation ran toward conifers and spotty undergrowth. It wouldn't be mistaken for the Andes or the high Sierras, but it made a change from sunbaked desert anyway. He had the camp staked out by nightfall, moved into position when full darkness cloaked the compound, pondering the way in which time seemed to slip away from him.

Three days in Baja, and Chris Stone was still alive, still bossing the militia remnants who had managed to survive their run-in with the Executioner. Bolan wasn't disgruntled by that fact, but it reminded him that he was running perilously short of time.

He got into position on the west side of the Zapatista camp, used the Beretta 93-R with its sound suppressor attached to drop a pair of sentries who were too close for comfort. This way they would have no opportunity to sound a warning to their comrades, and they couldn't cut off his retreat. Two birds with one stone, as it were—or with two bullets, in this case.

It didn't take him long to scout the camp. The place was built to house as many as two hundred men, but there were fewer than one-third that number currently in residence, as far as he could tell. That still made killer odds, but Bolan was adept at playing off bad numbers, turning them to his advantage with a little skill and strategy. If he could get the hardmen shooting at one another, Bolan thought, he would have come a long way toward solution of the numbers game.

To that end, he spent the next half hour moving cautiously around the camp, affixing plastic charges where he thought they would be most effective when it came to rattling his enemies. He wanted the guerrillas to believe they were surrounded, that they had to fight their way out of a trap. If he could pull it off, and make it all seem real enough to those inside the compound, they wouldn't be all that scrupulous in their identification of targets when it came to breaking out. Whoever stood between them and the haven they were looking for would be an enemy, someone to be disposed of by the most efficient means available.

When he had come full circle, back to where he started, Bolan spent a moment arming the explosive charges he had set on the perimeter. With the control box on his belt, they could be fired in unison or individually, according to his needs. The beam that set them off was undetectable to human ears, and operated over ranges up to and including half a mile.

But he would be a great deal closer when he blew those charges. Up close and personal, in fact, where he could read his enemies' reactions on their faces.

Any moment now.

He made a final scan around the Zapatista camp, was reaching for the detonator when he spotted a familiar face emerging from a hut that he had taken for the camp's command post. He had seen that face back at the ambush site, and was a bit surprised to see it here. No twins were involved; the bruise along the rebel's jawline told him that, together with the strained expression on his face. The man looked tired and worried, as if he had already glimpsed hell once that day and didn't care to get a closer look.

Tough luck.

Bolan watched the familiar face start giving orders, saw them carried out by younger men who snap-saluted and went to do his bidding without question, eagerly, anxious to please. He knew this man wasn't the founding leader of the Zapatistas—that prize target lived far to the south and east, between Oaxaca and Chiapas—but he also recognized this target as a man worth taking out. His loss would hurt the movement, maybe more than losing all the other men assembled in the camp together.

Bolan frowned and let his thumb settle on the detonator button at his waist.

"I DON'T CARE if you checked it once already," Altamiro snapped at one of his subordinates. "Go back right now, and—"

The first explosion sounded something like a hand grenade, but louder, echoing across the camp from the leader's left. He turned in that direction, squinting, even though the sun had long since dropped behind the western foothills, and the camp was dimly lit. Somewhere along the road of life, he had decided that a squint made him look thoughtful and determined, not unlike the great American, Clint Eastwood.

At the moment, though, it only made him look confused and worried, neither one of those a quality that would inspire a positive reaction from his men.

Altamiro couldn't see much from the direction of the blast, where smoke was hanging thick around ground zero. Something—was it one of the latrines?—had been demolished, and a number of his soldiers were advancing cautiously in that direction, closing in to check it out. The Zapatista captain hoped that it had been some kind of stupid accident—better a moron playing with a live grenade than enemies advancing on the camp—but all such hope was banished when a second blast erupted on the far side of the camp, directly opposite his quarters.

Two more explosions came immediately on the heels of the first two, and once again they echoed from opposite corners of the camp. Altamiro ruled out artillery, since there was nothing of the background noise big guns produced, none of the whistling scream that marked the falling shells. Even a mortar gave some muffled sound on launching its projectiles skyward, and the sights couldn't be readjusted quickly to allow for hits in widely separated quarters of the camp. That meant grenades or planted charges, and he didn't know offhand which would be worse. In either case, it meant the enemy was close.

Altamiro had changed his clothes since he returned to camp, put on a crisp new uniform, but he was still armed with the compact AR-18S, suspended from a shoulder strap. The side arm on his hip was a Colt .45, the vintage Army model, with most of its bluing worn off from much handling. It wasn't a flashy weapon, but it got the job done, and it had saved Aldo's life on more than one occasion.

"To the vehicles!" he shouted, already thinking of escape. And then, in case his thoughts were too transparent, he swiftly added, "We must not allow our enemies to seize the motor pool."

Four bodyguards fell into step around him, shielding their leader with their lives, as they were trained to do. When they had reached the vehicles, he would contrive some story as to why they should evacuate the compound. It wouldn't be difficult, considering his rank, the instinct of his soldiers for self-preservation and—

The motor pool went up when he was still some eighty yards away. It started with a single blast, then gasoline was spilling from a ruptured fuel tank, sparking, blazing, spreading. Other vehicles were catching fire as Altamiro stood there, watching dumbly, knowing that he could do nothing to prevent it. They had fire extinguishers in camp, but nothing that could handle conflagrations of such size and heat. In moments flat, a string of secondary detonations rocked the camp, gas tanks exploding, and he saw a flaming tire shoot out of the inferno, rolling free across the camp like some demented pyromaniac's plaything.

Altamiro clutched his automatic rifle in a firm two-handed grip, eyes searching for a target onto which he could project his rage. He felt as if he had been trapped in a recurring nightmare and couldn't awaken, even with the sounds of combat ringing in his ears.

Someone was shooting, the bullets flying wildly back and forth across the camp. From where he stood, the Zapatista captain couldn't tell if they were under fire from guns outside the camp, or if his own men had begun to fire at anything that moved. Their discipline wasn't the best, although they did all right in skirmishes where they could see the enemy, pick out uniforms and target them with rifle fire.

This kind of fight was very different, with the tables

turned, applying slick guerrilla tactics to the men who were supposed to use them. Worse, the timing helped confuse things, falling after dark, when it was difficult to see their adversaries and the worst of peasant superstitions were inclined to rear their ugly heads.

Another blast, away to Altamiro's right, took out the compact water tower, dropping it directly onto the communications hut, which flattened underneath the weight, its radios and other gear all shorting out like crazy in the sudden deluge. That was brilliant, almost making Altamiro laugh despite the rage that welled up in his throat, like bile. Whoever planned *that* blast was thinking with his brain and acting with his balls.

They had no wheels, no radio, and from the sound of echoing explosions, they were cut off on all sides. Right now, the first thing Altamiro needed was a place to hide.

"This way!" he snapped at his defenders, turning from the wreckage of the motor pool and moving back in the direction they had come from. "We have no more time to lose!"

RICO SILVA DIDN'T understand a bit of what was happening, why it was happening to him or why it had to happen now. He knew only that it had to stop, and soon, or he would lose his mind. The hammering explosions, punctuated by staccato bursts of gunfire, made him feel as if his skull were splitting open and his brain were being roasted on a spit. His ears rang painfully, and in his panic, Silva found that he could hardly breathe.

So much for training to become a bold guerrilla warrior.

He had gone through the training, run the courses, practiced with the several weapons that they showed him how to use. Guns didn't hurt his ears so much when he was firing them, but he was known to cheat sometimes, put little balls of cotton in his ears before he went off to the firing range. This night he had no cotton, and he wasn't shooting guns; the guns were being fired at him, with murderous intent. If that wasn't enough, the shattering explosions seemed to have no end, a new one ripping through the camp from yet another quarter while the blast before it was still echoing in Silva's brain. He tried to keep the noise out, tried to keep his thoughts coherent and in order like a soldier should.

He spotted Aldo Altamiro and four bodyguards from where he stood, across the compound. They were running toward the armory, supposedly the most secure building in the camp. It was the only one, in fact, that had a concrete floor, and while the walls were simply plywood layered with sheet metal, they had no windows. With a single door, the place was simply guarded; you could plant one man outside, and he could watch the compound's arsenal with no great difficulty.

Five men on the inside, though, was something else. They would have ample guns and ammunition with which to defend themselves, but Silva wondered how effective the windowless building would be as a fortress. One or two men could fire through the doorway, if they left it standing open, but the enemy could fire on them from every side at once. And if the bullets started coming through the walls...

Perhaps, Silva thought, his comrades merely wanted to collect more weapons for the fight. He had no reason to assume they were so foolish as to trap themselves inside the armory, especially with the explosions going off around them, seemingly without a pattern, tearing up the camp. He hoped they weren't that stupid, but he would have to find out for himself.

He needed leadership, and there was no one to provide it but Altamiro. Silva had been taking orders from the same man since he joined the Zapatista movement three years earlier, and while he didn't always understand the reasoning behind those orders, he was always happy to obey. It made life simpler when he didn't have to think of everything himself. Before the Zapatistas he had tried the army, but they had rejected him because he couldn't read or write. The rebels, when he found them, made no such distinctions. All you needed was the proper attitude, a will to fight and the ability to do as you were told.

He followed Altamiro now because there would be no one else to tell him where to go and what to do once he arrived there.

When he saw the stranger, tall and dark, pursuing Altamiro and the others at a distance, Silva had a flash of inspiration. This couldn't be the only enemy, but it was clearly one of them. If he, Rico Silva, could destroy this man who meant his leader harm, then it would prove his value as a soldier of the revolution. It shouldn't be difficult in the confusion. All he had to do was sneak up on the stranger's blind side, take good aim and drill him through the heart.

No problem.

Silva scuttled forward, clutching the Kalashnikov that felt as if it were carved from solid lead. Another moment, and he would be close enough to risk the shot. Two more, and he could hardly miss.

The stranger hesitated, staring at the armory as Altamiro and his men began to disappear inside. They left the door ajar, perhaps to watch the battlefield while they were stocking up on arms and ammunition. Silva didn't know and hardly cared just now, when he was on the scent of victory.

With thirty feet between him and the man he stalked, Silva stopped and stood his ground. He brought the AK-47 to his shoulder, sighting down the barrel at his prey, and realized that something was amiss. It would be easier to shoot the prowler in the back, but it felt wrong somehow. It made his skin crawl and his stomach churn.

All right, then. He would call out to the man and have him turn around. What could go wrong? He had the bastard covered with an automatic weapon. There was no way any man alive could beat those odds.

What should he say?

The more Silva thought about it, standing there, the more he was convinced that he would blow it if he hesitated any longer. Christ, he could say anything he wanted to! The man wouldn't survive to share his words of wisdom with the world in any case.

Sucking in a deep breath, Silva clutched his weapon almost painfully against his shoulder as he cried out, *"Alto, por favor!"*

THE WARNING SHOUT SAVED Bolan's life. He didn't think about it, didn't hesitate. The voice came from behind him, slightly to his right, and that was all the fix he needed on an enemy who was no more than forty feet away. The move required coordination, but you didn't have to be a double-jointed acrobat. A simple flexing of the knees, one ankle crossed behind the other while he swiveled at the hips, his upper body rotating from left to right. The M-16 went with him, leveled from the waist, and he was firing by the time he had completed one-fourth of the turn, the 5.56 mm tumblers spraying in a level arc some thirty feet across.

The Zapatista gunman should have had him, but he lost it due to poor reaction time. The guy was awkward, almost sluggish, and the Executioner's reaction to his challenge took him by surprise. Before the light of life winked out behind his eyes, he blinked at Bolan, trying to digest what had gone wrong.

Before his lifeless adversary hit the ground, Bolan had turned back toward the building where the man with the familiar face had disappeared. There were no windows, plus the slabs of rusty sheet metal nailed up around the structure told him it was something special by the rebels' standards, and he had to guess that was their arsenal. Too small to house a vehicle for five, it was constructed like a poor man's blockhouse, situated near the center of the compound for convenience—or for protection. That way, every soldier in the camp would have a fair shot at the hardware in emergencies, and all of them together could defend the Zapatista arms cache if it hit the fan.

There seemed to be no major move in that direction at the moment, though, as sentries on the camp's perimeter were busy trading shots with one another, firing at the shadows that surrounded them or cautiously perusing structures that had been destroyed by Bolan's C-4 charges. He couldn't count on the general distraction to last long, however, if he started dueling with the troops inside the makeshift armory.

He had to make it quick, aware before the thought took shape that nothing was more fluid than a plan devised in combat, when a thousand different variables could affect the outcome of the simplest strategy. Still, nothing ventured...

Bolan was advancing on his target when a gunner in the doorway saw him coming and began unloading on him with an automatic weapon. Some kind of submachine gun, probably 9 mm from the sound of it.

There was no time for stealth, then, he decided. His index finger found the trigger of the M-203 launcher mounted underneath the foregrip of his assault rifle. A gentle squeeze, no great recoil, and Bolan watched the doorway, with its winking muzzle-flashes, as the deadly canister flew straight and true.

The shock wave and successive detonations told him that he had been right about the building's function. Some kind of explosives had been stored there, and he now heard small-arms ammunition going off like deadly popcorn in the midst of the inferno. Different calibers made different sounds, the flaming hulk a minifirefight in itself.

The Zapatista guards were coming, but he didn't feel like lingering to meet them. He had dealt them a sufficient blow for now, depriving them at once of both their leader and their arsenal. The rebels were a sideshow to his main attraction anyway.

The Executioner had other fish to fry, another war to fight.

And it was waiting for him even now.

13

"I'm telling you, I didn't know about the woman when we talked last time. I just found about her my own self."

The lie came easily to Nehemiah Zinn, perhaps a sign that he was still a carnal sinner in God's eyes, but he preferred to view it as a talent that he utilized in Yahweh's service. Any fool could tell the plain, unvarnished truth, come rain or shine, and watch the world collapse around him. But it took an artist to devise the proper lie from righteous motives. Hell, a godly lie could be a thing of beauty.

And a thing of beauty was a joy forever.

Still, Zinn couldn't help but notice skepticism radiating from his one-man audience. Captain Rodriguez wasn't buying it about the woman, but at least he wasn't openly disputing Zinn, either. Maybe he was smarter than the pastor gave him credit for, with brains enough to pick the truth out of the lie and use it to his own advantage, let the rest go with the bathwater.

The woman was a threat to Stone, which also meant she was a threat to Zinn and everyone he dealt with. She was a Fed, for Christ's sake—beg your pardon, Father—and if she was left at large, allowed to file her report back in the States, there was no telling how much grief she could bring down upon their heads. Some kind of international incident, he wouldn't be surprised, and even someone like Rodriguez had to know what *that* would mean, his precious badge and tiny pension hanging by a thread.

Zinn would have gladly taken care of her himself, but he was no detective, and he had a few more problems on his hands right now. Like helping Stone find out who was responsible for all his recent casualties, and paying the Figueras brothers back for their resistance when he sent his men to raze their camp. Too many problems all at once, Zinn thought. It made him dizzy, thinking of the things that could go wrong and leave him stranded, holding one huge sack of smelly shit, but times like this were when you had to put your faith in Yahweh, let him share the burden and assist you in promoting his almighty truth.

Except it didn't seem to quite be working out that way. So far, the good guys had been taking all the major hits, while Yahweh's enemies kept coming out on top. It was a trial and tribulation, but it wouldn't last, of course. The Lord might move in mysterious ways, but once he got rolling on your ass, there was no stopping him. Next time, Zinn told himself. Next time.

And missed a comment from Rodriguez. "Say again?"

The captain didn't roll his eyes or grimace. He was too smart for that, insulting white men with connections.

"I believe you said this woman is an agent for the DEA?" Rodriguez said.

"That's right." Another lie, but what the hell? One Fed was just as bad as any other, agents of the decadent, Jew-dominated government in Washington who thought they were above the laws of God and man.

"Why was she after Señor Stone?" the captain asked. "I did not think the Paul Revere Militia was involved with drugs."

"They're not," Zinn answered. "The Feds are framing him, you follow me?"

"Yes, I understand."

The DEA routine had been an inspiration on Zinn's part. The Mexican police were famous for protecting drug dealers, down to the point of killing U.S. officers and knocking off their own presidential candidates in public shooting matches. It was one thing sure to get Rodriguez cooking on the case. Just watching him across the table with their coffee cups between them, Zinn could see the captain chewing on it, wondering what kind of praise he would receive from his superiors if he could flush a DEA sting down the drain.

"Where is this woman?" Rodriguez asked.

"I don't know," Zinn answered. "That's why I'm telling *you* about it, right? Stone had her, but the men who took his camp apart made off with her."

"She could be back across the border now," Rodriguez stated.

"In which case, you won't find her, will you? But it wouldn't hurt to look around some, would it?"

"No." The captain plainly didn't like Zinn's tone of voice, but there was little he could do about it in the circumstances. "I will begin to look for her at once."

"That's fine," Zinn said, allowing himself a smile. "One thing to keep in mind—she likes to snoop around and catch folks with their pants down, if you get my drift. Watch out for anybody snooping where they don't belong. She may not look exactly like the photograph."

Zinn wasn't sure why Stone had bothered with the Polaroid, since he had planned to kill the woman anyway, but it would come in handy now. Rodriguez had it in his pocket, reaching up to press one hand against the khaki fabric there, as if he were clinging to a cherished object.

"If she is in Baja, I will find her."

"I hope so," Zinn said. "I surely do. Because if you don't, there could be hell to pay."

THE TRICK OF GETTING information, Ginger Ross realized, was all in knowing whom to ask. And when you asked, it didn't hurt to have some ready cash on hand.

The money was a problem. She had lost everything when Stone evacuated the militia camp in Idaho and took her with him as his hostage. Thankfully she had a sister in Altoona who was sitting home when she called collect, and who agreed to wire five hundred dollars without asking tons of questions. The AmEx office in Punta Prieta was a tiny hole-in-the-wall operation, but it filled her needs. Ross paid her taxi off, acquired a cheap rental car and started hunting.

Now the hard part.

She remembered just enough of her high-school Spanish to sound like an ignorant tourist, but she made do with what she had, refusing to make things worse by fumbling with a phrase book. As she expected, most of those she met, particularly merchants, spoke sufficient English to get by and make a living from the tourist trade. A fair percentage of them actually spoke the language better than the average high-school senior in L.A., with more attention to the grammar and less emphasis on slang.

Communicating was one thing, however; getting answers to the kind of questions Ross had in mind was something else. A gringo couldn't simply stroll into a shop in Baja and inquire about the local gunrunners. Assuming that the locals even knew whom she was looking for—and many of them would; she felt that with a veteran cop's sixth sense—such people stayed alive and on the loose by clinging to their secrets as an old maid clings to her virginity. A combination of respect and fear, with bribes thrown in where necessary, would protect the kind of operation Ross was looking for.

Still, she and Jeff had done the groundwork before he disappeared. She knew most of the players—names and many of the faces from surveillance photos—so she wasn't starting cold. It was a "simple" question of convincing someone, somewhere, to direct her, tell her where the parties she was seeking could be found.

The day was getting on toward noon before she found the pimp. When stalking criminals, the best place to begin your search for information was with cops—or other criminals. Since she was barred from reaching out to the police on several counts—they might report her to the ATF, more likely to the very men she was pursuing—that left people on the other side. From there, she reasoned that a group of men like Stone's expatriates would feel a need for women sometime, while a combination of their circumstances and the racism that bred in most of the American militias would prevent them forming close romantic ties with any of the natives. That left kidnapping and rape as one potential outlet, which was fraught with peril for a bunch of gringos trying to be inconspicuous, or commerce with the local prostitutes.

The first pimp Ross met was slick at dodging questions, trying to recruit her for his stable, making noises like a man who might have information to exchange but ultimately coming up with nothing. By the time they parted, she was convinced that he knew nothing worth her time, and she regretted paying him the twenty dollars that had set him babbling in the first place.

Number two was different. He was every bit as oily as her first contact, but this one had a certain reticence about him, as she had come to expect from men who often knew too much for their own good. He made no serious attempt to turn her out, but rather listened to her questions, alternately frowning or attempting not to frown, occasionally nodding in a way that could mean anything or nothing. When he named a price, it was beyond her means, but everything in Mexico was subject to negotiation.

Finally they struck a bargain, and the pimp told her

where she could find Carmelo Obregon, a middleman between the Zapatista rebels and the Paul Revere Militia on their early arms deals. With any luck at all, she could persuade the middleman to tell her when and where the next exchange was scheduled. If she couldn't meet his price—and that was highly doubtful, after paying off the pimp—then she would have to squeeze him, catch him by the short and curlies to persuade her man that talking was the way to go.

And then what?

If and when she got the information she was seeking, what did Ross plan to do with it? Once more, she couldn't go to the police and count on any help from them. Likewise the ATF. She had been AWOL too damn long to look for anything but a suspension from her bosses, and the bureau had no jurisdiction over crimes in Mexico, regardless. That left her with two options: she could either face the bad guys on her own or give the operation to Belasko, let him handle it, perhaps convince him to let her participate.

Strike three. She didn't know where the man was, much less how to resume communication when it suited her and sell him on a plan that might not track with his agenda. She was sure of one thing, though: even if she could reach Belasko, he would never let her tag along on any mission where he thought there might be bloodshed.

Which brought Ross full circle, to her one and only plan. If she could find out when and where a meet was scheduled, she would have to play the rest of it by ear, perhaps acquire a camera somehow, and record the rendezvous on film or tape. And all for what?

She walked back to her rental car and slammed the driver's door behind her, venting some of her frustration on unfeeling metal. Ross knew what she would have to do; now all she needed was the nerve to see it through.

And luck, oh, yes, to see her out the other side alive.

THE CALL TO WASHINGTON was overdue, but Bolan still might have postponed it, if he hadn't gone back to the Rosarito safehouse and discovered that the lady Fed was gone. The risk had been a calculated one, leaving her there alone, but he wasn't her baby-sitter, and he couldn't keep an eye on Ross every moment of the day and evening. Bolan hoped that she had done the wise thing for a change, but he wouldn't have bet on it.

When he reached out to Hal Brognola, then, it was a multipurpose call. The scrambler Bolan carried could be easily attached to any touch-tone telephone, including the Executioner's mobile unit, which had satellite-relay capacity, eliminating any need for land lines. It wasn't without its problems—split-second delays between a comment being made on one end and received at the other, the ghost of an echo from Bolan's own voice—but it was virtually untraceable without triangulating gear that none of his local enemies possessed.

He called Brognola at his Justice Department office, down the road from the White House, directly opposite the FBI Building on Pennsylvania Avenue. It was a private line, connected to the outside world without the benefit of secretaries, and the big Fed used it only for the kind of urgent business that required utmost discretion. Possibly a dozen people in the world possessed that number, and no more than half of those had ever used it.

When he picked up on the second ring, his voice was flat, devoid of apprehension, expectation, curiosity. "Hello?"

"It's me." Bolan didn't have to ask if Brognola was scrambling the call. The private line was plugged into an automatic scrambler that immediately scanned and locked on to the frequency of whatever device was operating at the other end. Without that bit of high-tech wizardry in play, Brognola's greeting would have been an unintelligible grumble, and he wouldn't understand a word that Bolan said.

"You need to watch yourself down there," Brognola said. "I'm hearing things."

"I wouldn't be surprised. That's why I called."

"Word is, the Paul Reveres can take a licking, but they keep on ticking."

"With a little help from their friends," Bolan added.

"What else is new? You've got almost as much graft on the table where you are as anywhere in Bangkok or Hong Kong."

"It shows," Bolan said. "Did you know Pike's patriots were dealing with the Zapatistas?"

"Dealing what?" Brognola asked. Now he was curious, which told Bolan that he was also taken by surprise.

"Hardware. Cash-and-carry. From the looks of it, I'd say they're selling merchandise picked up from military bases, maybe even in transit from the manufacturer."

"Small arms?" Brognola asked.

"Mostly. Some grenade launchers and mines, M-60s, this and that. The ATF's been onto it, but there's not much for them to do, considering." By which he meant to say that Mexico was well beyond their jurisdiction, and the fix was obviously in big time.

"I don't suppose one of their people's trying, though?" Brognola said.

The question brought a frown to Bolan's face. "The truth is, I was hoping you could tell me that," he said. "I've lost touch with their player here."

"I'll have to ask around," Brognola said. "There's nothing on the grapevine to suggest that she's come home. I think they would have tipped me off, at least, if she was back on-line."

"That's what I was afraid of."

"Can you reestablish the communication?"

"Doubtful," Bolan replied. "If she's gone hunting on her own, she won't be leaving any bread crumbs on the trail."

"Too bad. But you did what you could."

That didn't sit well with the Executioner, but he had no immediate response. Instead, he changed the subject. "Stone and the militia have connections to some kind of weird religious commune here," he said. "A so-called prophet by the name of Nehemiah Zinn's in charge of that end, and he's feuding with some dissidents who bailed out of his congregation some time back."

"A holy war?" Brognola asked.

"The poor man's version. It's one more angle of attack."

"Whatever works," Brognola said. "But you're on shaky ground down there."

"I gathered that. How's Pike?"

"The last I heard, he's conscious, paralyzed from the neck down. Some kind of traffic accident, I understand."

Bolan replayed the moment in his head, the founding father of the Paul Revere Militia standing in his headlights, one arm raised as if the gesture could protect him from a speeding car.

"He should have used the crosswalk."

"I hear you. By the way, a certain first-term congressman is said to be behaving strangely. Burning bridges with his primary constituents, that kind of thing. You'd almost think somebody put the fear of God into him."

"Maybe he's maturing," Bolan said, remembering Neal Martz, the panicky expression on his face as Bolan questioned him.

"You never know. Stranger things have happened. Even so, I'm betting if he wins his next campaign, we'll see a different side of him. The classic politician, through and through."

"That's progress."

"Maybe," Brognola replied. "Some think so, anyway. Myself, I liked him better as he was. The enemy you know, and all that jazz."

Bolan decided that the congressman might rate another visit, once he had returned to the United States, but it was no emergency. He had more pressing matters on his mind right now.

"How are you doing on equipment?" Brognola asked.

"I'm all right for now. If I come up short, I'll take a shot at living off the land."

"If you need anything at all—"

"I have the number," Bolan said.

"Well, then..."

"Yeah, I'll see you."

Bolan and Brognola had never been much on goodbyes. Each knew how fragile life was, and while neither man was superstitious, they avoided any mention of a permanent farewell by mutual, unspoken agreement.

The soldier severed the connection, stowed his mobile telephone and put the car in gear. He had no leads on Ginger Ross, and there was nothing more that he could do to help her now. The lady Fed was on her own unless he picked up information on her movements somewhere down the line. Until then, if and when it happened, he had enemies lined up and waiting for a visit from the Executioner.

And Bolan didn't plan to keep them waiting long.

CAPTAIN RODRIGUEZ TOOK the phone call shortly after 1:00 p.m. He didn't recognize the voice, but knew the name at once when it was spoken. Despite his calculated blindness to the major criminals who operated underneath his very nose, Rodriguez had no problem with his memory for names and faces, details, facts and figures. He was by no means a stupid man, although he lacked formal education.

Experience had been his school, and he had learned his lessons well.

The call came from Punta Prieta, where the caller—one Lorenzo Cruz, a pimp and small-time marijuana dealer—sold his wares to Anglo tourists who were resolute enough to make it that far south of San Diego and Tijuana.

Cruz confirmed what Zinn had already predicted—namely that the woman whom Rodriguez sought was asking questions, though her inquiries appeared to make no sense for someone working with the gringo drug-enforcement unit. Rather, she was trying to locate Carmelo Obregon, a front man for the Zapatista underground.

The more he thought about it now, the more convinced Rodriguez was that Zinn had lied to him about the woman's job. Not that he cared, per se; it was *his* job to stop her meddling by any means available, no matter whom she worked for. Still, it rankled that the crazy gringo thought he could deceive Rodriguez, and that he wouldn't be caught in such a clumsy lie. It was another symptom of the prejudice Zinn and his cronies had toward ''greasers,'' that they felt themselves superior in all respects. In other circumstances, it would almost have been comical, but at the moment, facing so much death, the captain didn't feel like laughing.

He would help Zinn kill the woman. That much would be in his self-interest—to protect his job, the extra income he received each month in bribes—but he wasn't about to play the fool. Rodriguez meant to do the job *his* way, and to collect more information in the process, something he could use against the gringos when their time came.

And it would, the captain told himself. It always did for men like that. Somewhere along the way, they always made a slip, ran out of money, broke the rules of their agreement with the powers that be, and when that happened, he would be on hand to wield the sword of vengeance. Or the automatic rifle, as the case might be.

Just now, though, he had other fish to fry.

Rodriguez had no difficulty finding Obregon. Guerrero Negro was his home and base of operations, though he traveled widely throughout the peninsula on business, normally involving guns. The Zapatistas were his major customers, but Obregon was also known to deal with drug runners, bank robbers and all manner of criminals. From time to time, if there was nothing else to do, he even sold his wares to normal citizens, assuming they had the money he required and were inclined to circumvent the local firearms laws.

This week, Rodriguez learned, his quarry was doing business in Santa Inez, some eighty miles north of Punta Prieta. The captain telephoned ahead, had the man picked up by police on the scene. Obregon was waiting for him when he got there, in the basement of the local station house. They had a drink together—several drinks, in fact, warm sodas poured into the smuggler's nostrils while he was suspended upside down in manacles—and he agreed to help the lawmen spring their trap. It was the very least that he could do, all things considered, if he wanted to remain in business.

If he wanted to remain alive.

It was arranged for Obregon to let himself be seen around the city, taking care of business, acting as he would on any other day. Rodriguez and his men would shadow him, be waiting when the woman came to speak with him. They would arrest her if they could, deal with her privately, away from prying eyes, but if they had to kill her on the street, who would there be to challenge them? They were the police, after all. Their word was law.

And if Carmelo Obregon should happen to be cut down in the cross fire, well, so much the better. He was nothing but a criminal, in any case. Rodriguez owed him nothing, and would probably receive a commendation for eliminating him.

He had to smile at that, the way things worked sometimes. You started out on an obnoxious little errand for the gringos, and it wound up working out to your advantage in the end. And someday, maybe in the distant future, when Pastor Zinn and his associates wore out their welcome, then Rodriguez would be pleased to lead the raiding party that was sent to bring them in.

He hoped they would resist, at least a little bit, and give him the excuse he needed to annihilate them all. And when that golden day arrived, the captain would be pleased to play his part.

But for the moment, he would focus on the woman and Carmelo Obregon, the first links in the chain. They should expect no mercy from Rogelio Rodriguez when they stood before his guns, for he had none to spare.

SANTA INEZ WAS the end of the line. Ginger Ross had run her man to earth—the first of several, anyway—and now she had him spotted: short and slender, hair slicked back with too much oil, a thin mustache that could as easily have been a pencil mark as facial hair. He wore a cream-colored silk shirt and black slacks, with shoes so polished that they looked like patent leather.

She was a block behind Obregon when he stopped at an open-air cantina, took a table facing the street and ordered wine. Ross considered how to handle it and went for the direct approach. She sat down in the table's second chair, directly opposite her quarry, flashing him a smile that never reached her eyes.

"I know that you speak English," she informed him, skipping the amenities. "Don't even think of playing games, all right? And while we're on the subject, don't get up. I have a pistol pointed at your crotch.''

It wasn't strictly true, of course. The gun was in her handbag, on her lap, where she could reach it easily, but Ross wasn't aiming it at Obregon. Not yet. Still, what the man didn't know...

The weird part was, he didn't seem surprised to see her. There was something like resentment in his eyes, but he didn't react with anything approaching shock. Instead of studying her face, trying to figure out exactly what in hell was going on, he seemed to stare past her, checking out the street.

"What do you want?" he asked, and there was something in his voice that made her think he didn't really care.

She cursed herself and knew she should have seen it coming, following his gaze across the street, where two men dressed in khaki uniforms were just emerging from a shop directly opposite. Away to Ross's left, two more were stepping from an alley, and behind Obregon, to her right, another trio was unloading from a black sedan.

How had she missed the trap? Too late to think about that now. Obregon was on his feet, backing away from her. His chair tipped over, clattered on the pavement, and he had his hands up, thrust in front of him, palms outward, saying, "No, no, no!"

The first shot struck him in the palm of his left hand, drilled through and punched into his upper chest. Its impact threw him backward, but he still took two more bullets even as his reeling body toppled to the floor. Belatedly she heard a warning shouted from across the street and understood that this wasn't your ordinary bust. These policemen had shown up prepared to kill, and she was next.

She found the Ruger in her purse, scattered the other contents of the bag around her feet in drawing it and swung around to face the nearest pair of uniforms. Both officers were aiming pistols at her, lining up their shots, and there was no time to consider what it meant to fire on a policeman when they plainly meant to smoke her.

She didn't bother to aim, squeezed off one quick shot per man, the Ruger bucking in her fist. She was surprised to see the policeman on her left clutch at his thigh, blood pumping from between his fingers. Jesus, just like that, and several guns were blasting at her as she tipped over the wrought-iron table, ducked behind it, scuttling on her hands and knees into the shady darkness of the tavern.

They would follow her, of course—might have the rear staked out already—but she had to take the chance, do something, *anything*, to try to save herself.

A bullet chipped the tile beside her left hand, and she turned to fire another shot at her pursuers, knowing it was wasted even as she pulled the trigger, grateful for the flash and thunder even so.

A moment later, she had space to rise and run, out of the line of fire. A waiter loomed in front of her, and Ross hit him with an elbow, felt his nose crunch with the contact, dodging past him as he staggered backward, cursing her in Spanish.

Better luck next time.

The other patrons in the small cantina were recoiling from the sounds of gunfire in a panic, scattering in all directions, unintentionally helping the woman make her getaway. She cleared the bar, brushed through a swing door into the smallish, aromatic kitchen, headed for the alley out in back. The door was almost close enough to touch when it swung open, and another khaki uniform blocked her retreat. She had a glimpse of captain's bars, a bulky pistol rising in the man's hand.

They fired together, scalding pain in Ross's side, but she was quicker, conscious of the ugly little hole that suddenly appeared below one of her adversary's startled eyes. His head snapped back, and Ross nearly stumbled on his body, going out the door. The alley lay in shadow, but she looked in both directions, saw no other uniforms and took off running, lurching, to her left.

Her car was off in that direction, though she had no realistic hope of reaching it. And if she did, what then? The blood was soaking through her shirt already, and although she guessed the giddiness of shock was mostly her imagination—so far, anyway—she still had trouble staying on her feet.

How long before they cornered her and finished it?

What difference did it make?

She wished that she could speak to Belasko one more time, be sure that he would take care of unfinished business, but she was already long past hoping. Ross knew she would be lucky now if she could simply die a swift and relatively painless death.

But she kept running anyway.

What did she have to lose?

14

The bungalow with a Pacific view bore no resemblance to a hospital, nor would a casual observer have detected any evidence that it was fortified against attack. Bolan himself, if not directed to the hideout by an urgent summons, would have passed it by without a second glance. Whoever prepped the place had done a decent job.

That much was a relief, at least, as Bolan pulled his car into the graveled driveway. He had an Uzi on the vacant seat beside him, ready if the set turned out to be a trap, but at the moment, he was more concerned about what waited for him in the bungalow itself.

The callback from Brognola, coming barely half an hour after they had spoken on the scrambled line, was a distinct surprise. Brognola had a message from the ATF, that Ginger Ross had surfaced, gravely wounded, to make contact with an undercover agent on the job in El Rosario. The rest was hazy, but Brognola had compiled sufficient details to create at least a sketchy outline of the action.

Ross had apparently gone looking for a contact, someone with a connection to the Zapatistas, but she had to have left a trail along the way. A team of *federale* headhunters were waiting for her when she made her contact, ready to shoot first and save the questions for another time. At least two men were dead—her contact and an officer—but the woman had managed to escape the trap, with a bullet in her side, and reach out for the one man in the neighborhood who could be trusted to assist a gringo Fed in trouble.

Bolan parked his car some thirty feet from the bungalow and spent another moment studying the layout, half-expecting sniper fire from the surrounding trees. Instead, the front door opened and a husky, bearded Anglo showed himself, making no effort to conceal the shotgun at his side.

"You coming in or what?" he asked.

It was a short walk to the bungalow, but Bolan felt each step, aware that it could be his last. Brognola had assured him that the place would be secure, but things were happening with lightning speed in Baja, and the enemy, including various militia gringos who could pass for federal agents at a glance, might well have found the bungalow by now if they were getting help from the police. Still, Bolan knew it was a chance that he would have to take.

"You're Striker?" the bearded man asked, using Bolan's code name as supplied by Stony Man.

He nodded in reply. "And you are...?"

"Cunningham. Just call me Al."

"How is she?" Bolan asked.

"A damn sight tougher than she looks," Cunningham replied. "She lost a lot of blood, but nothing she can't handle. It was through and through, the doc said, so he cleaned the wound and stitched her up, gave her some plasma. What she needs right now is rest, without a pack of *federales* breathing down her neck."

"And will she get that here?"

"We're strictly off the books with this place," Cunningham assured him. "Look up need-to-know in the dictionary, and this is what you find."

"*She* knew about it," Bolan said, making no effort to conceal his doubts about the bungalow's security.

"Well, yeah... I mean, sometimes, when we've got people working on the q.t., outside lawful jurisdiction, they're supplied with certain information as a last-ditch option, just in case they have to pull the pin, you know?"

"You're DEA?"

"Hell, no! Those cowboys couldn't keep a secret if their lives depended on it, which is why they keep on getting smoked down here."

"I didn't think the ATF ran moles outside the States."

"You were right. She's through the living room and down the hallway to your left, the second bedroom."

"After you," Bolan said.

"Hey, whatever." With a shrug the man, who had effectively identified himself as working for the CIA, preceded Bolan, pausing long enough to close and bolt the door behind them, talking nonstop as they moved toward Ross's room.

"I wouldn't want to mess with this one, I can tell you. Well, I mean, I'd *want* to, but I'd rather keep my gear intact, if you get my drift. From what I hear, she dropped that *federale* captain like a sack of dirty laundry. Nailed a couple of his flunkies, too, I understand, but they'll survive. Too bad."

"They set her up."

"You're surprised? Money talks down here, my friend. Forget about your NAFTA bullshit and the drain on jobs. The only sucking sound you'll hear in Baja is the payoff money going into cops' and politicians' pockets. Everybody's greasing the machine down here, and I mean everybody."

"You're familiar with the Paul Revere Militia and their tie-in to the Zapatistas?"

"Does a buzzard have bad breath? Those crazy shits can talk about their patriotic duty all they want," Cunningham said. "Wade through the bullshit, and they're just another bunch of assholes looking out for number one."

"You're not a fan, I guess."

"Not so you'd notice. Here we are." The door was closed, and Bolan hesitated, but his escort said, "It's cool. I'll be out front if you need me."

Bolan watched him go, then turned the knob and stepped into the room where Ginger Ross lay in a narrow bed, her hair tousled on the pillow. She wore a baggy T-shirt, and the sheets and blankets were pulled up to her armpits.

"Hey," she said, "you're late."

"You got away from me."

"I had some things to do." Her voice was weak, as if the act of speaking used up her remaining store of energy.

"That's what I hear. Stone's people have the *federales* in their pocket."

"Now you tell me." Ross forced a smile. "One of them's dead, I guess."

"You could have joined him," Bolan countered.

"That wasn't in the play book," she replied. "I didn't want to kill a cop, though. Christ, I guess I've really had it now."

"They're telling me you should be safe here," Bolan said.

"Back home, I mean. Eight years. Some great career, eh? I guess a letter of reference is out of the question."

"It may not be that bad," he told her, doubting the words even as they passed his lips.

"It may be worse, you mean. I doubt they'll try to lock me up, but that's the good news. Jesus, what a mess!"

"Just take it one step at a time. Right now, you need to get your strength back."

"Right, so they can kick my sorry ass all over Washington. I hope you're doing better than I did."

"I'm getting by," he told her. "Still connecting dots, but I'll get there."

"I bet you will," she said. "If you run into Stone…"

"I'll give him your regards. That's a promise."

Her eyelids drooped, and Ross smiled again. It didn't seem so forced this time. "They've got me on some happy pills," she told him. "I could walk on broken glass and wouldn't feel a thing."

"Why don't you get some rest instead?"

"That's what the doctor ordered."

"It sounds like good advice," Bolan replied.

"Maybe I'll take it for a change."

"It couldn't hurt."

"Hey, will you drop around again sometime?"

"If you're still here."

"Or maybe when we get back to the States?"

"We'll see."

"I'll be expecting you," she said. "You owe me one...or I owe you. Whatever, just be there."

She was already dozing as he let himself out of the room and went in search of Cunningham. The man from Langley occupied a camp chair on the front porch of the bungalow, his shotgun braced across his knees.

"You *will* take care of her," Bolan said.

"That's why I'm here. Doc says another day or two, and she should be fit to travel. She'll be going back, I guess."

"I guess."

"So, what about yourself."

"That's need-to-know," Bolan said as he stepped down from the porch and started toward his car.

"Okay. You'll give them hell, though, right?"

Bolan said nothing as he slid behind the steering wheel, but he was thinking: that was the plan. Damn right.

"How could they *miss* her?" Stone demanded, pacing restlessly around the shaded patio.

"I didn't get the details," Zinn replied, a sour feeling in his stomach. "All I know for sure is that she capped Rodriguez. Stupid wetback couldn't even take her when she was right there in front of him.''

"We should have had our people there," Stone grumbled, popping knuckles as he paced.

"The *federales* don't like interference," Zinn reminded him.

"Hell, no! They'd rather have their officers gunned down and watch the shooter get away. I wouldn't be surprised to hear they all went out for a siesta afterward, and left the bodies lying in the street."

"She won't get far," Zinn said, attempting to console his nervous houseguest. "She was hit, they're sure of that. And bleeding bad, from what I understand."

"Not bad enough to stop her," Stone retorted. "If the bitch was dying, they'd have found her corpse by now."

"Where could she go?" Zinn asked, and wondered for a moment whether he was asking Stone or talking to himself.

"Where did she go the last time?" Stone demanded. "How the fuck do *I* know where she goes? You may remember that she's not alone in this, or did that slip your mind?"

Zinn felt the anger heating up his cheeks and swallowed down the smart-ass answer that would probably have set Stone off to raving. For an ice-cold mercenary, Stone appeared to have some problems in the nerve department. Or, Zinn wondered, was he simply running out of guts?

It sometimes happens to the best of them. A man could fight so many battles, wade through so much blood without a hitch, and then one day he simply couldn't take it anymore. Sometimes the weakness crept up on him slow, by degrees, and other times it came on all at once, like falling off a log and landing in deep shit. Whichever way it went, Zinn knew from personal experience with fighting men that you could rarely save a soldier once his nerve broke. Every now and then, one made a comeback, but most of them were hopeless, putting on a front for all the world to see, but cringing on the inside every time they thought of facing down an enemy.

Was that Stone's problem? And if so, could Zinn get rid of him before his weakness jeopardized the colony? There had been trouble ever since he came to Baja, getting worse each day. Zinn worried that another week would ruin everything that he had worked for all these years since he was forced to leave the States. It angered him to think that all his labor on behalf of Yahweh might be wasted, his best efforts shattered by a man who used to fight for money and was now unable even to perform that dishonorable trade.

"You might want to consider going somewhere else," Zinn said, attempting not to let the rancor come through in his tone.

Stone quit his pacing, stared at Zinn with cold, dead eyes, but kept his mouth shut. Maybe he was thinking that it wouldn't be a bad idea to bail out after all. Leave Zinn to take care of the problems he had caused, and find himself another place to hide, for all the good that it would do him. Dig the deepest hole on earth, and no man ever born could hide out from himself.

"Why don't you say what's on your mind?" Stone said at last.

"I just did. You've got someone on your case, we don't know who or why, and I got problems of my own, with the Figueras brothers and their people at Colonia Verdad. For all I know, with Pike gone, the militia may be finished."

Stone was glaring daggers at him, stalling for another moment, thinking of the perfect thing to say. "I'll make sure that the colonel knows you're so concerned."

"You tell him what you like," Zinn said, his right hand edging toward the Colt Commander on his hip. "Pike's paralyzed. For all I know, he's dying. Are you telling me *you* mean to run the show now that he's out of it?''

"I don't see any other volunteers."

"And *I* don't see who's picking up the tab," Zinn answered back. It felt good, standing up to Stone this way, instead of coddling him as if he were something special, better than the rest.

"What's that supposed to mean?" the mercenary challenged.

"Hell, we both know Pike recruited you for pay, to whip his ragtag army into shape. Are you denying that?" There was no answer from the pacing man. "All right, then. All I'm saying is, with Pike flat on his back and these damn people chasing you around like they're a pack of hounds and you're the rabbit, I don't see much profit in the whole thing for a man like you."

"I've got a job to do," Stone said.

"But not in Mexico."

"You're telling me to leave?"

"I'm asking you to think of what makes sense for all concerned," Zinn said. Now that his point was made, he could adopt a more conciliatory tone. "It makes no sense for you to bring all kinds of trouble down on those who never done you any harm."

"You're scared," Stone stated.

"I'm cautious. There's a difference."

"I don't see it."

"Well, now, maybe that's a problem in itself."

"Be careful, Nehemiah."

Zinn was smiling as his fingers curled around the Colt Commander's checkered grip. "You know me," he responded. "I'm a careful man."

Stone looked as if he was weighing up his options, finally deciding that it wouldn't pay for him to force a killing confrontation in the present circumstances. Maybe, Zinn reflected, he still had some sense left after all.

"I need some time," he said at last.

"Take all you need," Zinn told him. "Hell, we're all friends here. Take two, three days. Whatever."

"That's extremely generous."

"One of my failings," Zinn replied, relaxing now. "Give till it hurts, that's always been my way. Thing is, I don't know when to quit."

"I'll need to make arrangements for my people," Stone said.

"They can stay here if they like. 'Course, we have our rules, you understand. It's not free room and board, with no responsibility."

"I'll pass that on."

"And I'll be seeing you at supper, then."

"I wouldn't be surprised," Stone said.

STONE HATED to admit that Zinn had a point. In fact, he had been thinking long and hard about evacuating Baja when the self-styled "prophet" put it to him, sitting there and grinning with his fingers drumming on his pistol grip as if he were some kind of Old West gunfighter.

It would have been so easy, when he thought about it—two long strides across the flagstone patio, to grab the table by its edge and flip it over in Zinn's lap, pin down his gun hand while Stone reached across and slammed the knife edge of his hand across Zinn's larynx. Maybe he could drive the heel of one palm into the man's nose and send the bony splinters back through bloody eye sockets to find his brain...such as it was.

Of course, that wouldn't end Stone's problems. If he killed the preacher, he would have to deal with some of Zinn's disciples—maybe all of them—and he was short on soldiers for that kind of action. Better in the long run to let

Zinn think that he had won the day, back off with some vestige of dignity, and finalize his plans to split.

Stone was relieved that Zinn had agreed to let his handful of militiamen stay on. Without that small concession, Stone would have been forced to sneak away, slip past the guards with nothing but the camous on his back and disappear. He didn't give a damn what happened to the remnants of Pike's troops in Baja, but it made things more convenient for himself if he could shine them on with some bullshit about another mission, moving on to find them a replacement sanctuary for the camp that had been razed. He knew the men were stupid enough to buy it—had to be if they had stayed with the militia movement all this time, accepting the absurdities expounded by fanatics like Ralph Pike and Zinn.

The trick wouldn't be selling them a lie. The trick, Stone realized, would be in getting out of Mexico alive.

Because the enemy who had pursued him all the way from Idaho was still out there, still hunting. Ginger Ross, the Fed, was something else. The ATF or FBI would have to build a case, secure indictments, then arrest him if they meant to take Stone down. And by the time they went through all the procedures, he was confident that he would already have finished off his work for Rahman, banked his final paycheck and departed North America in search of friendlier surroundings.

With the other adversary, though, it was a pure survival game. Stone still had difficulty in believing that one man alone had brought him to his present state, wiped out so many of his soldiers, blitzed Pike's headquarters in Idaho, the camp in Baja. It was all but unbelievable. Stone knew that *he* couldn't have pulled it off alone, and he had always been the shining star in any training program that he joined, whatever military outfit he was part of, as a leader or a simple grunt, back in the ranks. He was an expert at his killing trade and had the references to prove it.

This was different, though.

The man—or men—who hunted him almost defied the laws of nature. Stone had taken pains to hide his tracks while fleeing from the States, but it had taken only—what, three days?—for Mr. X to track him down and butcher his men. Stone wasn't superstitious, but he was willing to admit that he had never met a soldier like the one—or ones— who had been dogging him.

All right, then. If he couldn't face the bastard in a stand-up fight and kick his ass into a shallow grave, then common sense told Stone he should bail out. He still had work to do for his employer, money to collect, but not in Baja. He had run to Mexico only to find himself some breathing room, a little respite from the heat. Now that the heat had followed him, there was no point in lingering with men like Nehemiah Zinn, whom he didn't respect.

The time to leave was now, tonight, before his phantom adversary had another chance to take him out. He would address the remnant of his troops, tell them he had a line on other quarters—maybe in Sonora—and that he was moving on to set up the arrangements with the *federales* there.

No sweat.

They would believe because they were conditioned to believe. More to the point, they wanted to believe. Toss them a bone, and they went away contented. They would sit and wait for him until it finally sank in that he had left them stranded, and by then the "prophet" would have put them all to work.

What happened after that was anybody's guess, and someone else's problem. Maybe the militiamen would rise against Zinn and his people, shoot it out with Nehemiah's "Christian soldiers" in a final blaze of glory. They would be outnumbered and outgunned, but what the hell? Who even cared how it turned out?

Stone would be well away by then. With any luck, his unknown stalker might remain in Baja, concentrate on Zinn and company, believing Stone to still be in the neighborhood. A few days would be all he needed, giving him the crucial edge.

But he needed to get out of there tonight. That much was crucial.

Stone walked back to his quarters, on the east side of the compound, wondering what he should pack.

The central compound at Colonia Cristo covered nearly six
acres, laid out in concentric circles that looked orderly and
well planned from a satellite's-eye view. Beyond the core
of the camp, Zinn's followers laid claim to roughly three
square miles of territory, with the compound centrally lo-
cated for convenience and defense. The land around the
tiny settlement was loosely guarded by patrols on horseback or in Jeeps. The latter vehicles were old, their bodies
rusted through in places, but they took Zinn's soldiers anywhere they had to go. As for the horses, Bolan wouldn't
venture to outrun one, but he could avoid them well enough
if he stayed on his toes.

The first thing he had done, in preparation for the strike,
was to eliminate all conscious thoughts of Ginger Ross
from his mind. If he went in there looking for revenge,
with anger guiding him, he wouldn't be at peak efficiency.
One slip could get him killed, and no one was more vul-
nerable to stupid mistakes than angry soldiers who were
thinking with their hearts instead of with their heads and
guts.

Ross was safe now, Bolan told himself, and she had paid
back the *federales* with interest for their ambush. It was
one more failure for his enemies, and the warrior had no
doubt that they were brooding over it right now. That gave
him the advantage, if they were distracted from the duties
at the compound, or if they were getting paranoid, jumping

at shadows in the night. Whatever took their minds off business gave him one more edge, another angle of attack.

Bolan parked well off the property and walked in from the north, all dressed in black, his face and hands obscured by war paint. He was carrying the M-16/M-203, together with his favorite side arms, 40 mm high-explosive rounds and frag grenades, a Ka-bar fighting knife and two garrotes.

The Executioner was literally dressed to kill.

He had no trouble dodging the patrols. The Jeeps were audible from better than a quarter mile away, with no competing noises to disguise their progress, and the horsemen worked in pairs, conversing back and forth as if they were out riding on a Sunday afternoon in Central Park instead of hunting in the darkness for an enemy who meant to see them dead. The horses might be able to detect his scent, Bolan thought, but if so, they gave no sign.

He was relieved that neither Stone nor Zinn had sent guards out with tracking dogs. That might have done the trick.

He reached the compound without incident, already wondering if it had been a tactical mistake to spare the guards who crossed his path out in the desert. He could probably have killed them all, but there had been a decent chance that one of them would get off a shot in the process, or that one of the patrolling horsemen would escape to rouse the camp.

He knew that it was coming up on 9:00 p.m., without referring to his wristwatch. Bolan had a knack for judging time, especially when he was living by the numbers, on a deadline, knowing that delays could cost him both the mission and his life. Instead of waiting for the camp to fall asleep, he would be moving in their midst, among them, taking maximum advantage of the darkness and a variation in role camouflage.

He couldn't pass as one of Zinn's disciples, dressed that

way, paint smeared on face and hands, but he could still wreak havoc in their camp, perhaps get close enough to drop their leaders at the start, before he wound up fighting for his life.

Despite the hazards he was facing, Bolan almost reveled in the prospect of a final confrontation with Chris Stone, solving the problem once and for all. If he could get to Nehemiah Zinn, as well, so much the better. After that, it would be open season on the tenants of Colonia Cristo— the men, at least—and while he questioned his ability to wipe out all of them, he meant to take a stab at it.

The compound proper was protected by a dozen sentries walking beats on the perimeter. If Zinn had detailed twice that number on guard duty, it would still have been no challenge, slipping past them while their backs were turned. A man could only do so much, defend so many yards of territory in the dark before he was reduced to simply killing time.

By nine-fifteen he had the compound scouted, major landmarks memorized, and he was ready to proceed. There was no sign of Stone or Zinn, and that was fine. Wherever they were holed up at the moment, they would have to show themselves when Bolan started kicking ass.

Another moment, yet, to get himself in place, and he was ready. He had his target chosen, with the M-203 launcher primed. The fireworks were about to start.

ZINN BELCHED and thought about the beef stew he'd just consumed. There was nothing better than a belly full of home-cooked food, unless it was a piece of tail.

Or victory.

He liked the way his showdown with the mercenary had resolved itself. It made him feel much better, more relaxed, that he had handled it as smoothly as he did. Zinn had expected Stone to balk, perhaps to challenge him, which would have meant a firefight in the middle of his colony. Zinn's people would have won, he calculated, but it would have been a bloody mess, regardless. Better for the whole community that Stone was leaving quietly, without a fuss.

Once he was gone, Zinn had a few ideas of what to do about his soldiers. He was close to the militia—or had been before he was compelled to leave the States—but there were times it pained him that the movement placed less emphasis on Yahweh than on guns and politics. Well, that would change, at least for those of Pike's men who continued to accept Zinn's hospitality at Colonia Cristo. They would quickly learn which side their bread was buttered on, and anyone who felt like arguing about the rules could take a hike.

The first explosion shook the ground beneath Zinn's camp chair, nearly toppling him into the dust. He bolted to his feet in time to see the shed that housed their generator blossom into yellow flame—and then the camp went dark, except for firelight coming from the source of the explosion.

Before Zinn took two steps, an automatic weapon opened up, away toward the north corner of the compound. He heard some of his people shouting questions back and forth, among themselves, attempting to discover what had happened.

The Figueras brothers!

They were striking back out of retaliation for the raid against Colonia Verdad. Of course! It all made sense now. They had been damn lucky, taking out his strike team, and it stood to reason they would try to follow up that bit of serendipity with payback for his effort to destroy them.

But what if he was wrong?

A second blast went off some distance from the first, one of his flatbed trucks exploding, rearing like a stallion at the rodeo, then settling back into a seething lake of fire. The gas tank blew a heartbeat later, and Zinn felt the heat against his face from where he stood, some fifty yards away.

Zinn knew he should be giving orders to his men, but he was tongue-tied, stunned to silence by the suddenness of the attack. He blinked his eyes, then slapped himself across the face, the stinging impact all it took to snap him out of it. He would have looked ridiculous if there was anybody watching him, but Zinn knew they were busy scrambling for their weapons.

For their lives.

He drew his .45 and started toward the burning flatbed, hoping for a shot at someone, any member of the raiding party. Whether it was the Figueras brothers or the people who were hunting Stone, he didn't know and didn't care.

"Vengeance is mine," Yahweh had said, but he would be forced to share this time.

Zinn had a feeling there would soon be blood enough to go around.

BOLAN UNLEASHED his third grenade and watched the south end of a Quonset hut collapse, as if a giant boot had slammed into the wall of corrugated metal. Smoke was pouring from the shattered windows as the door flew open, spilling half-dressed men into the night. Some of them carried weapons; others were involved with pulling on their pants or boots.

They could expect no mercy from the Executioner. He opened fire on them from thirty paces with his M-16, the 5.56 mm bullets drilling armed and unarmed targets with complete impartiality. The soldiers who were armed had no time to reply in kind; their comrades, meanwhile, barely understood their danger in the fleeting time before they were cut down. It was over in seconds, Bolan reaching for a fresh clip to replace the spent one that he had ejected from his rifle.

He was still no closer to Chris Stone or Nehemiah Zinn, despite all the damage he had caused in the first moments of his raid. They could be anywhere, and it would profit Bolan little to destroy Stone's troops if he allowed the mercenary to escape him one more time. The M-16 reloaded, Bolan thumbed another HE round into the launcher slung beneath its barrel and went hunting for fresh prey.

The sounds of gunfire and explosions had alerted sentries on patrol outside the camp, and they were rushing back to join the battle now, some driving Jeeps, the others riding horseback. Bolan saw a pair of mounted gunmen entering the compound to his left, both reining in their animals before the horses had a chance to shy and buck. The riders looked confused, and Bolan helped resolve their problem as he raised the automatic rifle to his shoulder, squeezing off two short precision bursts, clearing their saddles without harming either horse. The frightened animals gave out ungodly squeals and swung away from the explosive chaos of the camp, galloping headlong back into the desert night.

No one had spotted him as yet, and Bolan used the time to his advantage, squeezing off another HE round toward what appeared to be the colony's command post. There were no lights showing in the windows, and he doubted whether Zinn was there, but it made little difference. At the moment, Bolan's strategy was to unleash as much confusion and destruction as he could, raise hell with all the means at his disposal and destroy his enemies as they were flushed out of their holes. With any luck at all, one of them would turn out to be Chris Stone.

Bolan was just reloading the M-203 when a pair of headlights blazed in his face, one of the old patrol Jeeps running toward him on a dead collision course. There was no time to think, he made the call on instinct and adrenaline, cutting loose with both weapons at once from forty yards and closing.

The grenade was just a hair off target, slamming into the left front fender of the Jeep, when he had aimed it for the grille. As it exploded, Bolan's M-16 was stitching holes across the dusty windshield, painting startled faces red behind the glass. He took a long stride backward as the Jeep exploded, hit the deck in time to save himself from shrapnel winging overhead. The left front wheel was ripped free of its axle and went rolling past him, two or three feet from his elbow, trailing smoke and flame.

He didn't check the gunners in the capsized Jeep to see if they were still alive. It made no difference to him, one way or the other, just as long as they were neutralized. With that kind of crash, he seriously doubted whether either one of them would walk away, but he would leave it in the hands of Fate.

Bolan was moving toward another Quonset hut, with gunmen milling out in front, when someone on the far side of the compound spotted him and started pegging shots in his direction. He was no great marksman, missing by a yard or better on his first attempt, but Bolan didn't feel like giving him a chance to improve. Back to the deck he went, searching for muzzle-flashes in the shadows, picking out his adversary as the gunner fired another semiauto burst in rapid fire.

The range was close to eighty yards, and the Executioner had to give the shooter credit just for spotting him across the camp. Most likely, he was watching when the Jeep had charged at Bolan, saw him in the headlights' glare and witnessed the destruction of the vehicle. His plan to strike the big man from long range was a good one, but he had been hasty with his aim and blown the killing shot when he still had the critical advantage of surprise.

Now he was running out of time.

The M-203 belched a high-explosive round, and Bolan waited for the lethal canister to land. It exploded on impact, lighting up the target zone downrange. He saw his would-be killer reeling from the shock wave, going down on one knee, and he had the shooter lined up in his rifle sights before the flash of the explosion faded back to midnight blue. A smooth squeeze on the trigger, and a burst of half a dozen tumblers closed the gap between them, nailing Bolan's human target to the ground, his final tremors passing in the time it took to heave a sigh.

One more down, and he scrambled to his feet, reloading on the move. So many enemies, so little time.

And Bolan wasn't finished yet.

Not even close.

CHRIS STONE HAD USED UP every curse word that he knew, and he was starting to repeat himself. He had been packing when the first explosion sounded and the lights went out. Now he was fumbling in the dark and praying that he didn't leave out anything essential when he closed his bag.

He had his passports—three of them, in different names—his money belt, spare magazines for the Beretta 92-S in his shoulder holster, plus a box of loose 9 mm cartridges. His clothes and shaving gear were next, but he would have to do without them now. It was impossible for him to finish packing in the dark, and he was out of time in any case.

The bastards had come hunting him. Again.

Stone had no doubt as to the meaning of the racket in the camp. There was never any thought that the explosion might have been a gas leak, the resulting gunfire drawn from nervous guards on the perimeter. Stone had seen too much weird shit coming down in the past two weeks to cherish any hope that he would catch a lucky break at this stage of the game.

No way.

The duffel bag was flaccid, nearly empty, as he hoisted it across his shoulder, but Stone didn't mind. If he was going to be forced to fight his way out of the camp, he didn't need a load of socks and underwear to slow him. In fact, he could have ditched the bag entirely, stowed the contents in his pockets, but he didn't feel like wasting precious time when each new moment might turn out to be his last.

He stumbled through the darkness to the corner of his room where he had left the AK-47 standing upright, cocked and locked. Stone scooped it up and flicked off the safety, turning toward the doorway, moving cautiously to keep from running into any furniture. A few more steps and he would be there, on the threshold, poised to run.

He needed wheels and hoped the motor pool hadn't been torn apart by the explosions echoing across the compound. If he had to hike out, it would take him all night just to make it into Rosarito, and he would be forced to bag the first car he could find. Damn risky, with the *federales* on alert since they had had their asses kicked that afternoon, and he would rather not attempt it if he had a choice.

The door came open at his touch, and Stone smelled cordite in the air, raising the short hairs on his nape. It was an old, familiar smell that made him feel at home, from battlegrounds and firing ranges on four continents. He wasn't frightened by the firefight going on outside, but neither was he filled with rash bravado, like some green recruit who didn't realize that he was mortal. Stone had seen enough of sudden death—dispensed enough of it himself to know that no one was immune.

No matter how badly he wanted to survive.

He stepped into the smoky darkness, edging to his left, his back against the warm wall of the Quonset hut. His room had been divided from the quarters of his men by a plywood partition. Stone could hear them talking heatedly, one of them punctuating every sentence with four-letter words, but none of them was asking for him yet. It was as well that they didn't, since Stone had no intention of allowing anybody to divert him from his purpose. They could go to hell for all he cared.

As for Chris Stone, he planned on making tracks.

The compound's motor pool was still intact, as far as he could see, with no fires in that direction. Most of the sporadic gunfire came from the north side of the camp, while Zinn corralled his vehicles to the southeast. If Stone was quick enough, and no one intercepted him along the way, he had a chance.

But only that.

Nothing was guaranteed once bullets started flying. He had learned that lesson at an early age, and learned it well. Whatever happened in the next few moments, he would owe as much to luck as skill or strategy.

But sometimes soldiers made their own luck in the field. He knew that lesson, too.

With grim determination on his face, Stone broke from cover, moving swiftly toward the line of darkened vehicles almost one hundred yards away.

THE GUNMEN CLUSTERED in front of the Quonset hut were twisting, jerking, falling as a storm of 5.56 mm manglers ripped into their bodies, dropping them in tangled heaps. They fell together, some of them, like dancers sprawling from exhaustion in the middle of a marathon, while others tried to run for it, a couple firing aimless shots behind them as they fled.

But they were out of time.

Death tracked them from the shadows, squeezing off short bursts of almost surgical precision from his M-16. Bolan didn't count the bodies as they fell; their numbers held no interest for him. He would know when he was done, when no one moved upon the field of battle, and the only noise beside his footsteps crunching sand and gravel was the rippling, crackling sound of hungry flames.

There was still no end of targets around him. Bolan had to pick and choose; he couldn't simply unload on them all, kill everyone at once. A part of living through the raid wasn't only eliminating his opponents, but preventing them from killing him. To that end, the Executioner still required a fair degree of stealth, even when certain members of the home team had already spotted him and tried to take him out.

He palmed a frag grenade, released the pin, wound up the pitch and let the bomb fly across the compound toward a hut where two young riflemen were breaking out spare guns and passing them to unarmed friends. Apparently the bulk of Zinn's disciples weren't armed around the clock, which helped explain the relatively easy going he had had so far.

The main advantage of a hand grenade over the 40 mm launcher was that it gave Bolan's enemies no warning of their fate—no sound or muzzle-flash that would alert them, nothing that allowed them to escape. One moment, they were standing in a huddle, two men passing out the weapons, others reaching out for them with eager hands. The next moment, a smoky thunderclap erupted in their midst, and they were vaulting backward, broken bodies somersaulting through the air to land in crumpled heaps.

He followed up the hand grenade immediately with a 40 mm high-explosive round. It sizzled through the open doorway of the compound's arsenal and detonated when it struck a pile of wooden crates inside. Bolan could probably have guessed the caliber of ammunition that was burning from the sound of rapid-fire reports, but he had better things to do as members of the colony raced desperately to organize a fire brigade.

Good luck.

The Executioner moved on. His chief targets were still at large, still somewhere in the camp, and it would all have been for nothing if he let them slip away.

The smoky darkness covered him and saw him on his way.

16

Zinn had collected half a dozen of his own men, plus three more of Stone's who had been wandering around the compound, seeking their elusive captain. They had been confused, disoriented, and they offered no objections when the pastor ordered them to fall in with his men for mutual defense. It was encouraging, in fact, how easily the trio of militiamen had yielded to his will.

Now all Zinn had to do was stay alive so he could try the same trick on the others, make them his, once Stone was gone. Assuming any more of them survived the night.

Which wasn't guaranteed, by any means, the way things had been going since the first explosion rocked the camp. Zinn's whole community was on the verge of chaos—no, strike that, it was beyond the verge and well into the freaking twilight zone. Zinn found it difficult to get his bearings, even though the camp was built to his design. It all seemed different now, with crumpled structures burning in the night, smoke drifting like a pall across the compound, bodies scattered everywhere. Most of the dead were his; they had to be, since Stone had brought only a dozen-odd militiamen to the community when he arrived a few days earlier.

Dear God in heaven, had it only been a few days?

Zinn bit his lip to keep from taking Yahweh's name in vain. He didn't understand how all his years of work could

come to this, undone in moments by a man or group of
men he did not even know—and all for what?

Stone's fault, Zinn told himself. They were all right until
he came along and brought his trouble with him!

That thought helped give the man focus, gave him one
more enemy to search for, one whom he would recognize
on sight. There could be trouble with the three militiamen
if they were present when he cornered Stone, but Zinn
would have to deal with one glitch at a time. First, let him
find the bastard, then he was prepared to do whatever might
be necessary to eliminate the problem once and for all.

Zinn clutched the shotgun he had lifted from a dead man
and double-checked the safety, making sure that it was off.
He knew there was a live round in the chamber, and he
didn't want any delays when it was time for him to use the
weapon in his own defense.

Or for revenge.

In front of him, some seventy or eighty yards away, a
Jeep came weaving through the camp. Zinn saw one of his
people dodge in front of it, too slow to make the cut. The
right front fender clipped the runner, rolled him up and
dumped him off to one side in the dust, like roadkill.

Stone? Zinn couldn't tell, but he wasn't about to take a
chance on letting the militia captain wriggle through his
net. He snapped the shotgun to his shoulder, index finger
curled around the trigger as he bawled instructions to his
men.

"Stop him!" Zinn shouted. "Everybody!"

"But…he's one of ours," someone protested.

"He's running *over* ours, you idiot!" Zinn barked without a backward glance, his full attention focused on the
shotgun's sights and his speeding target. "Now, do like I
say!"

He aimed between the Jeep's bright headlights and a little higher, going for the windshield, squeezing off a blast

of shot before the others raised their guns. Zinn pumped the shotgun's slide and fired a second round, then his companions were unloading on the vehicle, as well, a righteous firing squad for Yahweh. By the time Stone's people saw him slumped behind the steering wheel, shot full of holes, there would be nothing they could do about it.

By his third shot, Zinn could see the Jeep was slowing, the driver slumping like a rag doll in his seat. The vehicle began to drift off course, losing momentum, veering toward a nearby bungalow. Zinn fired a parting blast into the driver's side and watched him topple over, then the Jeep collided with the building in its path and died, the engine stalling out.

Zinn led the charge, his scattergun with one live round remaining, and the Colt Commander on his hip to back it up. There was no question of the driver's fighting back, with half his face blown off and six or seven bloody wounds apparent on his torso. Zinn reached forward, grabbed the dead man's collar, dragging him upright, and saw—

One of his own disciples, Alan something. Names escaped him in his fury and confusion. Alan was a teenager, his parents saved about five years ago, impressed enough with what they heard from Zinn's pulpit that they followed him to Baja, Alan's daddy giving up the service station he had owned in Nashville. They were childless now, if they were even still alive, and wasn't that the shits?

"Who is it?" one of Stone's militiamen inquired.

"Nobody," Zinn replied. And that was true, at least. A dead man was the very definition of nobody. "Come along," he snapped. "We still got plenty work to do."

THE 40 MM HE ROUND exploded underneath the compound's water tower, shearing off two of the bulbous structure's wooden legs. For just a moment, the tower seemed prepared to stand there as it was, defying all the laws of physics, but it finally surrendered to the pull of gravity and toppled in slow motion to the ground.

Beneath it, firing from the hip at Bolan's shadow-shape, one of the compound's sentries felt death coming for him, glanced up just in time to see some giant object blotting out the stars and screamed before the tower flattened him, sheet metal bursting at the seams on impact, unleashing a mini-tidal wave.

The Executioner turned away, reloading on the move, and found that he had used up two-thirds of his 40 mm rounds. He could have guessed that just as well by looking at the wreckage of the compound, but the heat of battle had prevented him from counting as he went along. Still, there were plenty left, Bolan thought, plus the hand grenades, his side arms, spare mags for the M-16. Worst-case scenario, he could start taking weapons from the dead.

Hardware wasn't his problem at the moment. Rather, he had blazed a path halfway around Zinn's colony without encountering the man or Chris Stone. The more time that elapsed, the greater Bolan's risk that one or both of them would slip away—and of the two, he was primarily concerned with tagging Stone.

Bolan scanned the shadows, noting furtive movement almost everywhere he turned. Instead of firing on the shapes at random, he tried to put himself inside Stone's head, think as the mercenary would, anticipate the move that would make or break him.

Short of mounting an all-out counterattack, which seemed unlikely in the circumstances, Stone would have his mind set on escaping from the compound, leaving Zinn and company to take the heat, perhaps distract his enemies while Stone pulled off his getaway.

Unless he meant to hike out through the desert, Stone would need a set of wheels. Some of the vehicles in camp were grouped together at the southeast corner of the property, beyond the mess hall, but that still left several others—like the flatbed truck he had blown up—deployed around the compound. With luck and the ignition keys, Stone could take off in any one of them, perhaps change wheels in Rosarito or keep driving until he felt he was safe.

Too many bets to cover all at once, so Bolan played the odds. If he could only strike in one direction at a time, he would take out as many vehicles as possible.

He turned around and started for the compound's motor pool.

CHRIS STONE WAS FEELING lucky. For the first time since they bagged the lady Fed in Idaho, he had a feeling that perhaps Dame Fortune might be smiling at him for a change, instead of giving him the finger. He couldn't be sure, of course, until he put the camp behind him, shook the dust of Baja from his clothes and got on with his business.

Screw the enemy, whoever he turned out to be. Zinn would distract the bastard long enough for Stone to clear the killing ground, and after that it wouldn't matter. Let the crazy bastard track him back to the United States. So what? It would require a miracle for anyone to find him and derail his plans before he staged the final coup and banked his last big payoff from Afif Rahman.

It startled and disturbed Stone that he had begun to think about his enemy as *he* instead of *them.* Survivors of the early raids had been unanimous in fingering a solitary gunman, but it made no sense, the sheer amount of carnage he had caused. Still, Stone wasn't above believing anything right now. Survival was his first priority, regardless of the odds against him. Whether it was one man or a hundred bent on killing him, he had to get away.

A scarecrow figure staggered out in front of him, emerging from the shadow of a Quonset hut that served Zinn's people as a barracks. Stone was ready with the AK-47, tightening his index finger on the trigger, when he recognized the man as one of his. They didn't know each other well, but Stone never forgot a face. This one had lived through the attack that killed so many others just several nights before, and here he was again, back in the middle of the same old shit.

"Captain! Don't shoot! It's me, Bob Matthews!"

Stone relaxed his grip on the Kalashnikov, but only by a fraction. There was no one he could trust inside Colonia Cristo right now, no one who could assist him in escaping. They would only slow him down, reduce his chances of survival.

"Are we getting out, sir?"

"No," Stone said, "not *we*."

A 3-round burst from the Kalashnikov tore through the young man's chest and slammed him over backward, left him writhing in the sand. Stone didn't waste the time it would have taken for a mercy round to finish him. If Matthews survived his chest wound, he would be a hero. If he didn't, well, fuck him.

It was every man for himself, and screw the stragglers. Pure survival of the fittest, kill or be killed, do or die. This wasn't combat, with a goal worth dying for; it was a massacre, with Stone's people on the receiving end, and that made all the difference in the world.

There was a time it would have galled Stone, running out like this, abandoning his comrades, but he didn't need a string around his finger to remind him times had changed. This firefight hadn't been his choice, and those he meant to leave behind weren't his friends by any stretch of the imagination. They were simply pawns in a game they didn't even understand.

Another fifty, sixty paces remained before he reached the

motor pool and started checking vehicles for keys. Zinn normally collected them and kept them all in his command post, but there was a chance he had slipped up this time. If not, Stone knew how to hot-wire cars and trucks, especially the older models, which were all Zinn's cult was able to afford. It would require more time, but he could pull it off—provided that nobody intercepted him and killed him first.

He halved the distance to his destination, and was down to thirty paces, give or take. A bullet whispered by his face, and Stone dropped to a crouch, spent several precious moments looking for a sniper, finally deciding it had been a stray round rather than a purposeful attempt to take him out. He straightened, kept moving, focused on his goal, but still alert to any danger from behind him or on his flanks.

He reached the motor pool and started to check the ignition switches, striking out on six vehicles out of six. No problem. He was underneath the dashboard of a '69 Ford station wagon, fiddling with the wires, when he was startled by a burst of automatic gunfire close at hand. Much closer than the rest, in fact.

Stone peeked above the dashboard, caught a glimpse of Nehemiah Zinn and several others huddled ten or twelve yards from the motor pool, unloading on a tall man standing farther out. It took a moment in the firelight for him to identify the solitary shooter, but Stone's eye for faces didn't let him down.

Belasko! Mike Belasko, damn it! Stone had guessed that he was dead in Idaho, or maybe caught a break and fled the Paul Revere headquarters while the firefight was going down. Now here he was again, decked out in camouflage fatigues and war paint, packing heavy weapons, dueling toe-to-toe with Zinn and company.

Stone knew his adversary in a heartbeat, felt like grabbing the Kalashnikov and wasting him right there, but he was worried that the traitor might not be alone.

He bent back to his work beneath the dashboard, cursing to himself, and focused on the problem of escaping with his life.

BOLAN HAD SPOTTED Stone as he approached the motor pool. A moment later, Nehemiah Zinn and several of his men had caught sight of the Executioner, recognized him as a stranger in their compound and opened fire.

Their haste had saved his life, the first rounds going high and wide. There was no place to hide, so the warrior stood his ground and started giving back the hostile fire in kind, his own nerves steadier, his marksmanship a product of his need, plus long experience.

Zinn had nine gunners with him, lined up like some kind of sloppy firing squad, and they unloaded all at once with semiauto rifles and handguns. They had enough firepower to wipe him out, but they were nervous, jumpy and none too expert with the weapons they were carrying. That combination—haste and mediocre skills—gave Bolan one last lease on life.

He raked the line from left to right, unloading with a HE 40 mm round when he had reached the middle of the group. Already, two or three of his assailants had begun to break and run, deciding that discretion was the better part of valor, but the impulse came too late for them to save themselves.

On Bolan's left, two of the gunners went down kicking, gut-shot by his M-16, both still alive but well out of the fight. A third man stopped two rounds below his sternum, blinked at the Executioner once in dull surprise, then toppled forward on his face, stone-dead before he hit the ground.

The high-explosive round went off just then, scattering

his remaining enemies as if they were toy soldiers slapped aside by some ill-tempered giant in a sudden fit of pique. One did a midair somersault and landed on his back, with all the boneless grace of a dead fish. Four others hit the deck in awkward attitudes, but they were clearly still alive, though some had picked up shards of shrapnel in the process. Two more managed to stay upright, breaking for the nearest cover—the motor pool—with ungainly strides.

Bolan was tracking them when he remembered Stone, the blaze of headlights bringing his quarry back to mind. A station wagon was spewing dust behind it as the rear wheels dug for traction, then the big machine sprang forward, aimed for the warrior on a hard collision course— with his two human targets in the way.

One of them threw himself aside and missed the charging juggernaut, but his companion wasn't fast enough. The station wagon hit him squarely, rolled his body up across the hood, where his skull cracked the windshield, leaving crimson smears behind as gravity took over and he tumbled off the left side of the speeding vehicle.

There was no time for Bolan to reload his grenade launcher, only time for him to spray the station wagon with his M-16 and hope he scored a luck hit on man or machine. He saw the vehicle taking hits, divots appearing on the hood, a portion of the bloody windshield blowing inward, but the vehicle kept coming, holding steady on its course. At last he had to leap aside, and even that was nearly not enough, the driver making an attempt to swerve and nail him.

The right front fender grazed Bolan's boot while he was airborne, slamming him through a painful shoulder roll that ended with him on his knees and shouldering the M-16, prepared to chase the station wagon with a parting burst. He squeezed the trigger, cursing as the hammer snapped down on an empty chamber. Taillights winked at him almost insolently as the old car disappeared into the night.

He struggled to his feet, expecting pain from his right ankle, pleased that there was none to speak of. Bolan fed the M-16 another magazine and started to check out the bodies scattered in the no-man's-land between him and the motor pool, stopping when he found Nehemiah Zinn.

The man groaned when Bolan slapped his face, but that was all.

It was enough.

Bolan threw Zinn across his shoulder in a fireman's carry and retreated into darkness, carrying the only trophy he would claim that night.

17

Stone reasoned that the Feds might have a cordon waiting for him at Tijuana, maybe stretching east to Mexicali. With an eye toward minimizing problems, he dipped into petty cash and hired a boat at San Felipe, making the crossing to Puerto Peñasco in just under two hours. Halfway there, he shot the master of the boat, together with his teenage mate, and tossed their bodies overboard.

No witnesses, no case.

Nobody seemed to notice when a gringo docked the old boat by himself, although they may have seen it in and out of port a hundred times with other hands on deck. In Mexico, especially along the border, where the drug dealers plied their trade, most residents were smart enough to mind their own business, keep their mouths shut and wake up the next day, safe and sound. They learned by the example of their neighbors who had failed to recognize the sacred right of privacy, and who had suffered grievously as a result.

Instead of checking with the harbor master, as required by law, Stone left the boat tied up and walked directly to the nearest used-car lot, where he unloaded more of his money for a rusty junker that still had some life underneath the hood. Before he left Puerto Peñasco, Stone also purchased cans of extra gasoline and canvas water bags, some cheese, tortillas and dried meat. It was a madman's shopping list, but Stone knew what he wanted, and the local merchants didn't argue with a gringo who was so free with his money.

When he had laid in his supplies, Stone started driving—not on Highway 8 to Sonoita, as his enemies would guess—but east, across the unforgiving desert on a one-lane blacktop ribbon, until he picked up Highway 2. The highway took him through Tajito, Pitiquito and a string of other small towns, all more or less the same, until he started north again on Highway 15 to Nogales.

They could still be waiting for him there, Stone realized, but it was far less likely than along the California border. In these days of budget battles, cutbacks in "unnecessary" spending, there was no way Uncle Sam would cover the entire 1,500-odd miles of Mexican border effectively. Not searching for one man.

And not this soon.

For all he knew, his enemies were still tied up at Rosarito, maybe searching for his body in the ruins of Colonia Cristo. Hell, it was even possible that Zinn had gotten lucky, scored a hit on Stone's determined stalkers.

He recalled his last glimpse of the colony, and something told him that the mess had only gone from bad to worse once he was out of there. It would have been a miracle if Zinn had rolled up the bastard, where Stone himself had failed—and the merc didn't believe in miracles.

Belasko. That was something. Thinking that the bastard had come that close, had actually gone out on a raid with him back in the States, gave Stone the creeps. Belasko could have nailed him anytime, but he had delayed the move, waited until the time was right. Just when Stone had the lady Fed wrapped up, in fact...

Stone tried to puzzle out the link between those two, but he was having trouble with the logic. On the one hand, he had Ginger Ross, clearly an agent for the FBI or ATF. On the other hand, Belasko came in blasting like the trailers for an Arnold Schwarzenegger movie, blood and thunder all the way. No mention of a warrant, reading anyone his rights or taking prisoners, not even back in Idaho, on good old U.S. soil.

So, what the hell was this?

Stone had no answer for that pressing question, and it didn't matter how he turned the damn thing upside down or inside out. It made no sense from any point of view, this new approach to tackling the militia problem by annihilating the participants. He thought the Feds had learned their lesson after Ruby Ridge and Waco, showing their new tolerance for brain-dead zombies in the so-called Freeman stand-off one year after Oklahoma City. Now here you had some wild man shooting up the countryside and killing dozens, scores of people, not only in the American Midwest, but also in Mexico.

His short list of concerns included two items, and only two. First up, he had to survive and hang on to his liberty at any cost, no matter what it took. And second, he had to try to finish off the job Afif Rahman was paying him so handsomely to execute. Indeed, success at number two would go a long way toward ensuring his success with number one. If everything went down all right from that point on, there was a chance he could persuade the Arab's backers to provide him with a sunny sanctuary. Someplace in the Middle East, perhaps, as they had done for Carlos, way back when.

The Middle East would only be a temporary resting place, of course, a pit stop on his way to bigger, better things. Stone didn't love the desert all that much, with oil derricks pumping night and day, like scrawny dinosaurs feeding if you looked at them just right in silhouette. No, thank you very much.

The heat was fine—he didn't mind the sun a bit—but Stone would go for someplace tropic if he had a choice.

Maybe somewhere in South America, or maybe the Carib-
bean. He could even try the South Pacific, *really* stretch
those dollars on some island where the women wore less
clothes than dancers at the Crazy Horse in Vegas, and the
men were always looking for a chance to share their wives.
A smaller version of Tahiti, and he would be a smaller,
smarter Marlon Brando, playing Mr. Christian with the
heathens.

Before he started living out his fantasy, however, Stone
would have to nail down the final payment. Which meant
that he would have to do his job.

He thought about the Seabee motto, from his father's
war: "The difficult we do at once. The impossible takes a
little longer."

Right, then. If it took a little longer to complete his mission, Rahman could learn patience. All those Eastern types
were said to be half-mystic, anyway. The course Stone had
selected for himself was difficult, but not impossible.

He would get started on it right away.

FROM WHERE HE STOOD—or *sat,* to be precise—Nehemiah
Zinn wouldn't have said that he had gotten lucky. Quite
the opposite, in fact. He would have said, with all apologies
to Yahweh, that his ass was up Shit Creek without a paddle.

It was a headache, literally, trying to remember what had
happened in the camp before his world blacked out and he
woke up again in what appeared to be an old, abandoned
warehouse. Zinn had fleeting mental images of gunfire, he
and several of his men unloading on a tall, dark stranger
in the middle of the compound, hitting him with everything
they had before the mother of all bombs went off and
dumped him on his ass.

Or on his head, more like it, from the way he felt. Zinn
still had no idea exactly what had happened, but the puzzle
pieces he could see were plain enough. He was a prisoner

somewhere outside Colonia Cristo. His keeper was the same man Zinn had been intent on killing just before it all went blank.

"You missed," the stranger said, regarding him from twelve or fifteen feet away.

"I see that," Zinn replied.

He also saw that he was seated in a straight-backed wooden chair, hands bound behind him with what felt like baling wire, his ankles similarly fastened to the front legs of the chair. He wouldn't quite reach the floor, which meant Zinn couldn't even tip the chair in protest if he wanted to.

And it was just as well, he thought as he considered his surroundings, since the floor was made of concrete. A man could break his neck or bust his skull wide open on that kind of surface, even falling from a relatively modest height. It was much better for the moment if he simply waited, found out what the stranger wanted from him.

He was still alive, and that news had to be encouraging, since Zinn's assailant could as easily have finished him back at the compound, put a bullet through his head while he was down and out. The very fact of his survival told Zinn that he had something the stranger needed, which in turn made him feel powerful. Except that he was trussed up in a chair and couldn't move, of course.

"You killed my people," Zinn remarked by way of making conversation.

"Some of them," the stranger granted.

"Can I ask you why?"

"Of course," the stranger said, and that was all. The silence hung between them for a moment, thickening.

Zinn finally made out what his enemy was waiting for, and said, "So, why'd you do it?"

"Mostly I was after Stone. He got away from me again. That's three times now. I have a hunch you might know where he's going."

"Sorry, I can't help you," Zinn replied. "I didn't exactly have a chance to log his flight plan, if you follow me."

"Okay," his captor said. "I'll buy that. Now, suppose you just run down the list of all the places where he *might* go to hide out or look for reinforcements. Wrap that up for me, and we'll call it a night."

Zinn puzzled over that one for a moment. Granted, he knew some militia camps, safehouses and the like, where Stone could no doubt find a temporary haven, but he wasn't sure that he knew all of them. Ralph Pike could be close-mouthed, and Stone was a chip off the old block, despite the fact that they weren't related. What if he went on to name a dozen hideouts, and his captor wasn't satisfied?

Torture.

Zinn felt his scrotum shrivel, and his stomach started to twist into knots. No, not his stomach—farther down. He curled his toes so tightly that a charley horse bit into one leg, and clenched his sphincter muscles in an effort to control his bowels. God, if he soiled himself, how would he live with the humiliation?

More important, though, how would he live if he refused to talk?

"You ask a lot," he told the big man, stalling.

"Not so much. You're dealing for your life."

"And if I don't talk? What's the deal?"

Zinn's captor reached under one arm and drew a pistol. It resembled a Beretta from the future, with an extended magazine, a sound suppressor in place, some kind of metal switch or lever fastened to the front part of the trigger guard.

"If you won't talk," the big man said, "then you're no good to me at all."

Zinn didn't need the gift of prophecy to work out what would happen if he refused to play along. That pistol obviously held a lot of rounds, and it defied all logic to believe his captor would be merciful, go for a killing shot the first time out. Would it be elbows? Shoulders? Knees? Perhaps the groin?

"I know some places," Zinn allowed, "but there could be some more I don't know, if you get my drift. I'm friends with Pike—at least, I was—but Ralph would never trust his mama knowing everything. You follow me?"

"So far. Let's hear about the places that you do know."

"Sure. Why not?"

Zinn talked for three-quarters of an hour, until his tongue and throat went dry, describing various militia sites and rattling off the highway numbers, names of county roads, the landmarks you could use to tell when you were getting close. He had to guess militia strength for any given place, since it was always changing. Zinn had doubts that even Pike could say precisely what the numbers were, much less how many of his men would stick if it came down to all-out war.

His captor sat and listened, didn't bother taking notes, which made Zinn guess the place was wired for sound somehow. Maybe they had a camera pointed at him right that very minute. In the States, that would have blown their case, the photographic evidence of a coerced confession, but he wasn't really telling anything about himself, and they had all these different rules in Mexico. For all Zinn knew, this was your standard grilling by the *federales,* when it slipped their mind that you had paid them long and well to look the other way.

This guy was an American, however, which told Zinn that he wasn't concerned with building up a legal case. That came as no surprise, considering the hell he had been raising back at the colony. Worse, it made Zinn wonder if he had been duped, if he had spilled his guts for nothing, and the stranger meant to kill him anyway.

"One more thing," the big man said, after Zinn had finished his travelogue.

"What's that?"

"You put the hit out on the woman, right?" his keeper asked.

"Not me. No, sir."

The big man kept on talking as if Zinn had not replied. "At first, I thought it might have been Chris Stone," he said, "but then it hit me that he wouldn't have the right connections, since he hadn't been here long enough. *You* have the right connections, though. I'd bet your life on it."

Zinn thought about his options for a moment, wondering if he should try to bluff it out with bullshit, finally deciding that he would fare better in the long run with a rough approximation of the truth. "It wasn't my idea," he said. "Stone told me she could hurt us if she got back to the States. I knew Rodriguez. There was nothing I could do."

"Too bad," the big man said.

"Well, hey…shit happens, right?"

"I know exactly what you mean," the stranger said, raising the pistol.

HE LEFT ZINN in the warehouse, put a padlock on the door and drove away. Someone would find him in a day or two—or maybe not.

It made no difference either way to Bolan. He was confident that Zinn had spilled his guts on the militia hideouts he had seen or heard described by people in the know. The Baja end of it was done—or would be, once the Company put Ginger Ross on a flight to the United States. Whatever happened to the lady Fed from there was out of Bolan's hands. He wished her well, and let it go at that.

Chris Stone was running free, and Bolan had to concentrate on that if he was going to complete his mission, neutralize the danger posed by members of the Paul Revere

Militia. He couldn't assume that Stone was simply looking for a place to hide, although he might be at the moment. Either way, the mercenary was a target he couldn't ignore. Back in the States, Stone was more dangerous than ever, maybe leaning toward retaliation for the setbacks he had suffered recently at Bolan's hands.

Their eyes had locked for just a moment back at Colonia Cristo, and Bolan thought it was a safe bet that his enemy had recognized him, even underneath the war paint. That was fine—hell, it might even work to his advantage if it made Stone sweat or increased his paranoia. In any case, he couldn't change it now.

As Bolan drove, he thought about the list of targets Zinn had given him. The man knew about militia camps or hide-outs in nine states, and six of those had more than one potential target for the Executioner. The trick would be to narrow down the list, pick out a handful of the best prospects—ideally, trim it down to one—and go from there. If he was forced to check the whole list by himself, it would take days or weeks. Stone would have time to travel several times around the world and work whatever mischief he already had in mind before Bolan could find him.

If he ever did.

It was infuriating, the idea of losing Stone again when he had been so close. Not once, but several times now, Bolan had come near enough to smell his quarry, but the merc was always one short step ahead of him, enough to make the difference.

Bolan thought about the time that they had spent together back in Idaho, the opportunities for smoking Stone that he allowed to pass because it wasn't time yet. He hadn't possessed the crucial information, wasn't ready to begin his sweep on the militia, needed just a little more to put him at the starting gate.

The next time he had a shot at Stone, he'd be in the bag.

The problem, obviously, was that he might never have that shot. In baseball parlance, he had already struck out, three swings without a hit. Of course, this wasn't baseball—wasn't any kind of friendly game at all—and there were no set rules. The winner was the man who walked away and left his adversaries dead or dying on the battlefield. In a "sport" like that, there were no playoffs and no semifinals. Every game was the World Series, and the only bonus coming to the winners was another day of life on Planet Earth.

It was a tough game, but for Bolan, it was still the only one in town.

He was already halfway to the border when his mood changed, and he caught his second wind. It wasn't hopeless yet, he realized. Not even close. He could reach out to Stony Man, ask for their help and try to narrow down his shopping list of targets.

It was something, anyway, and it would have to do.

The Executioner was hunting human prey, and he wouldn't allow himself another miss.

The game was going on, and Bolan had already bet his life on the result.

Next time, he vowed.

Next time.

* * * * *

Don't miss the exciting conclusion of
THE AMERICA TRILOGY.
Look for the Executioner #224,
CALL TO ARMS, in August.

When terrorism strikes too close
to home...

DON PENDLETON'S

THE EXECUTIONER®

THE
AMERICAN
TRILOGY

CALL TO ARMS

The pursuit of a paramilitary group terrorizing America
now brings Mack Bolan to the Everglades, where a
collaborating force of ultraconservatives is unleashing
an all-out assault against their homeland.

But a greater conspiracy lies beneath the violence that's
sweeping across America. One of her patriotic sons
has betrayed his country to Middle Eastern enemies,
who are pulling the strings of their U.S. puppets.

The penalty for treason is death. Mack Bolan is
the Executioner.

Available August 1997
wherever Gold Eagle books are sold.

James Axler

OUTLANDERS™

Trained by the ruling elite of post-holocaust America as a pureheart warrior, Kane is an enemy of the order he once served. He knows of his father's fate, he's seen firsthand the penalties, and yet a deep-rooted instinct drives him on to search for the truth. An exile to the hellzones, an outcast, Kane is the focus of a deadly hunt. But with brother-in-arms Grant, and Brigid Baptiste, keeper of the archives, he's sworn to light the dark past...and the world's fate. New clues hint that a terrifying piece of the puzzle is buried in the heart of Asia, where a descendant of the Great Khan wields awesome powers....

Available September 1997,
wherever Gold Eagle books are sold.

**East meets West in the deadliest conspiracy
of the modern world**

DON PENDLETON's

MACK BOLAN®

CODE OF BUSHIDO

Accused of the most brutal terrorist strike in U.S. history, a cadre of Arab radicals is set to go on trial in Chicago, even as angry Americans demand blood retribution. Mack Bolan brought down these killers, and now he must keep them alive to see justice served.

But when the terrorists escape in a holocaust of fire and death, Bolan picks up the tendrils of a dark conspiracy that reaches all the way to the Far East. The Executioner must battle the shogun of a new Imperial Japan—a man who masterminded a deadly plot to bring America to its knees.

Available in August 1997 at your favorite retail outlet.

**Don't miss out on the action in these titles featuring
THE EXECUTIONER®, STONY MAN™ and SUPERBOLAN®!**